THE HOUSE OF FEAR

Other books by the author

The Stone Door (novel)
The Hearing Trumpet (novel)
The Seventh Horse and Other Tales

Leonora Carrington
THE HOUSE OF FEAR
Notes from Down Below

Introduction by Marina Warner
Translations by Kathrine Talbot and Marina Warner

E. P. DUTTON NEW YORK

Copyright © 1988 by Leonora Carrington
Introduction copyright © 1988 by Marina Warner
Notes and compilation copyright © 1988 by E. P. Dutton
Translation copyright © 1988 by Leonora Carrington
Leonora Carrington's stories "The House of Fear," "The Oval Lady,"
"The Debutante," "A Man in Love," and "The Royal Summons" were
published in French, in slightly different form, in the volume
La Débutante *© 1978 by Éditions Flammarion.*
Leonora Carrington's story "Uncle Sam Carrington" originally appeared in
French under the title "L'Oncle Sam Carrington" in the volume
La Dame ovale *in 1939.*
"Préface ou Loplop Présente la Mariée du Vent" by Max Ernst
© 1939 by Max Ernst
Translation © 1988 by Marina Warner

All rights reserved. Printed in the U.S.A.

No part of this publication may be reproduced or transmitted in any form or by any means, electronic or mechanical, including photocopy, recording, or any information storage and retrieval system now known or to be invented, without permission in writing from the publisher, except by a reviewer who wishes to quote brief passages in connection with a review written for inclusion in a magazine, newspaper, or broadcast.

Published in the United States by E. P. Dutton,
a division of NAL Penguin Inc.,
2 Park Avenue, New York, N.Y. 10016.
Published simultaneously in Canada by
Fitzhenry and Whiteside, Limited, Toronto.

Library of Congress Cataloging-in-Publication Data
Carrington, Leonora, 1917–
The house of fear.
Contents: The house of fear—The oval lady—
The debutante—[etc.]
I. Title.
PR6053.A6965A6   1988   813   88-3907
ISBN: 0-525-24648-7

Designed by Steven N. Stathakis

1 3 5 7 9 10 8 6 4 2

First Edition

Collages by Max Ernst reproduced with the permission of the
Estate of Max Ernst.
Leonora Carrington's illustrations for **Down Below** *copyright ©*
Leonora Carrington

Excerpts from the poetry of Charles Baudelaire are from **Paris Spleen 1869**
copyright © 1947, 1955, 1962, 1970 by New Directions Publishing
Corporation. Translated by Louise Varese. Reprinted by permission.

Contents

Introduction *by Marina Warner* 1

THE HOUSE OF FEAR
Preface *by Max Ernst* 25
The House of Fear 27

THE OVAL LADY
The Oval Lady 37
The Debutante 44
The Royal Summons 49
A Man in Love 55
Uncle Sam Carrington 61

LITTLE FRANCIS
Little Francis 69

DOWN BELOW
Down Below 163
Postscript 1987 210

A Note on the Texts 215

12 pages of illustrations follow page 148.

THE HOUSE OF FEAR

Introduction

As a treat to celebrate her first communion, Leonora Carrington was taken to the small local zoo at the English seaside resort of Blackpool. She remembers it partly because it was the first time she had been to a zoo and seen the wild animals who occupied much of her dream time, and partly too because her mother took her. This was a rare treat, as the child was usually attended by her nanny. Creatures—actual and fantastic, wild and tame—populate Leonora Carrington's paintings, her sculptures, her stories and novels; she was "born loving them," and when she was living in Mexico, she responded with recognition to the Indian belief that each one of us possesses an animal—*nahual*—soul as well as a human one. In everybody, she says, there is "an inner bestiary."

When she was small, she was frightened of ghosts but not at all afraid of the "very funny" visions she sometimes had, in which a wild tortoise would sometimes cross her path or "an absolutely huge cat" would appear "sitting in a disused dog kennel." She began writing and illustrating stories very young, when she was around four years old. She dismisses the practise now—"all children do it."

The bestiary continued to inhabit her, and of all the animals within, the horse predominates, and next to the horse, the hyena. Both appear in her self-portrait of around 1937–1938, *The Inn of the Dawn Horse*, which shows the twenty-year-old girl sitting in jodhpurs and hacking jacket as if about to go out riding, while a hyena bitch approaches her, her udders full of milk. On the wall behind them a white rocking horse hangs, while through the draped window beyond, another escapes into a receding *allée* of trees. The rocking horse's lower jaw is missing, perhaps broken by the bit; but its living alter ego, galloping away in the green distance, is entire.

In "The Debutante," which Leonora wrote around the same time, the hyena becomes the narrator's friend and takes her place at her coming out dance; her stench alerts the guests at the dinner party of her imposture. Animal hairiness, animal smells mark Leonora's selves in several of the stories written between 1937 and 1943, and the plays and other tales which follow. "The Neutral Man" comments on the narrator's resemblance to a horse, while in *The Baa Lambs' Holiday*, a drama written in 1939, signs of creatureliness characterize the heroine, Theodora, and her chosen love, a werewolf born "laughing like a hyena and snapping at the soft red hands of the midwife."

The hyena embodies the young woman's sex and fertility, the horse her dynamism and speed and sovereignty. "A horse gets mixed up with one's body . . . it gives energy and power," Leonora Carrington says. "I used to think I could turn myself into a horse." She remembers how her mother told her stories about Jack Frost, the folk spirit of winter, who knew powerful magic, and how subsequently she, Leonora, pestered the subpostmistress in the village, through whom telephone calls had to be placed in those days, with requests to put her through to Jack Frost, who "would help change her into a horse." In *Little Francis*, the novella written in 1938 and published here for the first time in its original English, the image of the horse changes in tone and meaning. Francis finds he has grown a horse's head when Uncle Ubriaco, whom he loves, has abandoned him; equine nature brands Francis as an outcast from the universe of human exchanges. Spellbound, in animal shape, like Ulysses's men under Circe's wand, his outer form reflects his interior truth. "Animals are beautiful because they are naked—on the inside too," wrote Georges Hugnet, the Surrealist photographer and poet. When Francis is exposed to shame and pain, despair and ridicule, he too becomes naked, and the metaphor for that nakedness is his new-grown horse's head.

Leonora and her mother were the only members of the family to ride. Her three brothers and her father didn't, though they were sporting and liked nothing better than to "kill" fish and birds. (To her shame today, she used to go hunting too.) Leonora had a Shetland pony, Black Bess, who makes an appearance in the novel *The Stone Door*. After Black Bess died, Leonora was given a chestnut mare, Winkie. The family were brought up in a Lancashire mansion called Crookhey Hall, and though they left it in 1927, when she was a child of ten, for a somewhat less magnificent establishment, it is Crookhey (Crackwood in the stories), with its gardeners and huntsmen and maids and "lavatory Gothic architecture," which has provided the principal stuff of Carrington's art.

Her mother, Mairi, née Moorhead, was Irish, the daughter of a country doctor from County Westmeath, and "a complete mythologist" who wove tall tales about the family, discovering connections far and wide, from Maria Edgeworth to Franz Joseph of Austria. Leonora remembers a portrait of him turning into an "ancestor." Her father, Harold Carrington, was a textile tycoon who sold the family company, Carrington Cottons, to Courtaulds and became a principal shareholder of Imperial Chemicals Industries (ICI). His father had been a mill hand with a brilliant flair for invention. He had patented a new attachment to a loom which led to the development of Viyella, a blended wool every English child knows for its salutary properties of warmth, lightness, and durability.

The Carringtons were northerners, entrepreneurial, rough and ready, and unconventional. "You know what my father was most like?" says Leonora now. "A *mafioso*." By contrast, the Moorheads were fabulists: Catholic, intuitive, and easygoing. Between them, they wove the web of Leonora's imagination: Mairi read aloud the books of her favourite Irish writer, James Stephens, and the droll, dry tone of *The Crock of Gold*, the balance it achieves between whimsical humour and authentic spiritual questing, influenced Leonora's writing profoundly. Her father preferred the yarns of W. W. Jacobs—Gothic tales like *The Monkey's Paw*—and again, Leonora turned to good account Jacobs's mix of macabre black magic and English heartiness. She read the traditional English repertory of Beatrix Potter, Lewis Carroll, and Edward Lear, learned French from a mam'selle from France and ghost stories from her Irish nanny, Mary Kavanagh, who was the daughter of a prison warder and had joined the family as a sewing maid at the age of sixteen or seventeen. Nanny stayed through thick and thin: it was she who was sent out in 1940 in a submarine to fetch Leonora back from the asylum she describes in *Down Below*.

Leonora Carrington herself likes to puncture any illusions about the wealth in her background; she prefers to recall that Moorhead is a gypsy name, and a very common one in County Westmeath. Nevertheless, according to the custom of the English upper classes, Leonora was sent away to boarding school, where she was unruly. With the help of the bishop of Lancaster, she was then moved to a second Catholic convent, in Berkshire, but again the nuns could not cope. They thought there was something wrong with her, because she could write with both hands and preferred to write with her left, backward. (She still practises mirror writing, and she paints ambidextrously, sometimes with both hands at the same time.) After this further expulsion, she was sent to Italy to be "finished" at Miss Penrose's academy in Florence, where she came into contact with the artists who have influenced her painting most, inspiring her sequential storytelling, her use of tempera, and her love of cinnabar, vermilion, and golden, burned umber and earth colours: the Sienese masters of the trecento and quattrocento—Sassetta, Francesco di Giorgio, and Giovanni di Paolo. Her father thought painting "horrible and idiotic" and that "you didn't do art—if you did, you were either poor or homosexual, which were more or less the same sort of crime."

On her return to England she "came out," was presented at court in the last year of George V's reign, and given a debutante dance at the Ritz: the background of some of her stories. The season's round of pleasure failed, however, to distract her from her desire to paint, and at her insistence she was sent to a private academy, the influential art school founded by Amédée Ozenfant. It was 1936, the Surrealists were showing in London for the first time, and her mother gave her a copy of Herbert Read's *Surrealism*. The picture on the cover, Max Ernst's *Two Children Menaced by Nightingale*, struck straight into her. Today she recalls the feeling, "like a burning, inside; you know how when something really touches you, it feels like burning."

She was learning to draw chez Ozenfant and is still glad of the discipline he taught, but she was already painting from her fantasy, quite differently from any other pupil at the school. The same year Max Ernst was in London for an exhibition of his work, and he was introduced to Leonora Carrington, then aged nineteen, at a dinner given by the architect Erno Goldfinger, whose wife, Ursula, was a friend of Leonora's at the Ozenfant school. Ernst was forty-six, the Surrealist movement's "Bird Superior," eclipsing all others in fame and prestige with his effortless gaiety and cruelty of invention, his unstinting ability to replenish the store of fantasies and improvise new media, new methods. André Breton, the founder and formulator of the movement, recognized in Ernst the fulfillment of his ambitions for Surrealism in the visual arts. He invoked him as "the most magnificently haunted brain of our times" (*Le cerveau le plus magnifiquement hanté de nos jours*). Ernst conjured into art the doctrine Breton had proclaimed in the first manifesto: "Anything that is marvellous is beautiful, indeed only the marvellous is beautiful." (*N'importe quel merveilleux est beau, il n'y a même que le merveilleux qui soit beau.*)

Leonora Carrington was a very striking young woman, with her oval face and black eyes, her long black hair and slender limbs; in her artlessness and innate, innocent perversity she seemed to have sprung out of the dreamworld as if directly summoned by the voices of the Surrealists at their automatic séances, a real-life *femme-enfant* who speaks of desire and has not yet grown up enough to grasp the full implication of what she says. Belief in the penetrating faculty of youth, the young woman-child's closeness to mystery and sexuality formed the crux of Surrealist doctrine. In *L'amour fou*, for instance, Breton wrote a concluding letter to his newborn daughter: "Let me believe that you will be ready then [on her sixteenth birthday] to embody the eternal power of woman, the only power before which I have ever bowed." To Breton the *femme-enfant* was a figure of salvation, because "in her and only her there seems to me to dwell, in a state of absolute transparency, the *other* prism of sight, which we stubbornly refuse to take into account, because it obeys laws which are very different, and which male despotism must prevent at all costs from being divulged." She was the "*conducteur merveilleusement magnétique*," the "*seule capable de rédimer cette époque sauvage*" (the "marvellously magnetic conductor," the "only one capable of retrieving that age of wildness"). Max Ernst, in the autobiographical texts collected in *Beyond Painting*, recalled dreams teeming with young women, and in his frottages and collages he created imaginary beings such as "the beautiful gardener," "the nymph Echo," "Perturbation, my sister," and Marceline-Marie, "the little girl who dreams of entering Carmel."

Migrating into the forms of horses, hyenas, and other creatures of the wilds, mediating dreams of strange and disquieting desire, Leonora fulfilled the Surrealist fantasy of the child-medium who excites the lover's imagination and moves him to fresher, stronger visions. Ernst recognized his "bride of the wind," the mating mare he had drawn in the *Histoire naturelle* of eleven years before, as he revealed in the foreword to Leonora's story *The House of Fear*. They left England to live together in France.

Leonora Carrington and Max Ernst first rented an apartment in Paris, but conflicts with Marie-Berthe Aurenche, Ernst's wife, who was quite naturally furious about their ménage, as well as political quarrels within the turbulent Surrealist movement drove them south, and they settled in the village of Saint-Martin-d'Ardèche in Provence in the summer of 1937. *Little Francis* narrates the events of that summer and autumn, transforming Ernst into the figure of Uncle Ubriaco (Drunken Uncle), the Bicycle King with eyes like blue fishes; his wife, Marie-Berthe, into the odious and possessive pious daughter, Amelia; and Leonora herself into Little Francis. The novella was written in English that winter, in an exercise book with very few corrections, after Ernst had abandoned Leonora in Saint-Martin to rejoin his distraught wife in Paris, in the same way as Uncle Ubriaco cycles off without explanations, leaving Francis to fend for himself.

The text speaks with an authentic voice of forsakenness and communicates the experience of the nymph and love object from within; it testifies to the *femme-enfant*'s predicament, though the macabre denouement imagines a rather more extreme end for the stricken protagonist than eventually came about. In life Ernst, after painful and public scenes, eventually returned to Leonora. Leonora, looking back on those days now, cannot credit that she directed her anger against Marie-Berthe, rather than against Max Ernst, but on one occasion, when Leonora had joined him in Paris and his wife came upon them together in a café, Leonora leapt up and struck Marie-Berthe with all her force. Parts of *Little Francis* as well as the short story "Waiting," with its vision of women fighting and its scene of sexual jealousy in a soiled bedroom, dramatise these incidents. Leonora's passion for Ernst prevented her from seeing anything from Marie-Berthe's point of view. Instead she identified with Ernst's sense of victimisation by his nagging wife, to the extent that she imagines, in *Little Francis*, her own death at her hands. Recalling that time now, Leonora wonders at her warped sense of allegiance with a deep sense of regret.

The struggles and passions of that time, reproduced in *Little Francis* and some of the short stories, foreshadow the more acute breakdown Leonora suffered in 1940, described in the autobiographical text *Down Below*. She had wanted to enter the house of fear, but she had not expected that its doors would close on her so ineluctably.

During the winter when Ernst left her in Saint-Martin to sort out what Francis calls his "genital responsibilities," Leonora was taken in by Alphonsine, the local café proprietress, the Rosaline of the novella. "I didn't think he'd ever come back, I didn't know where I was going. I was like a monster. At least I felt like some sort of performing animal, a bear with a ring in its nose. I was *l'Anglaise,* and the café, which never had anyone in it, became crowded." She transforms this experience in *Little Francis,* adding the story of the bullfighter who seduces a woman in order to satisfy his nose fetishism and then embellishes her nose with tattoos and a ring. She says now of such experience, "I think it's death practise."

Little Francis can be read as a roman à clef: Francis looked at Uncle Ubriaco in the nude and "felt slightly sad as he watched him: he felt he would never love anybody so much." The novella is the story of an affair, and it gives the pleasures and the pangs of a true love story. Many of the other characters are also recognizable. The dreaming invalid Jerome Jones was inspired by Joë Bousquet (1897–1950), a poet and man of letters who lived in Carcassonne. He had been severely wounded in the First World War and did indeed smoke opium. Pfoebe Pfadade was based on a Hungarian fellow student at the Amédée Ozenfant Academy who energetically courted Max Ernst, and her father, the marquis de Pfadade, recalls another marquis for whom Leonora never felt the Surrealists' admiration; Egres Lepereff was inspired by Serge Chermayeff, the Bauhaus architect who had been asked by Leonora's parents to keep an eye on her in London and so brought down her youthful vengeance on his head. But such anecdotal reading seriously reduces the originality and imaginativeness of most texts, this one included. As Leonora herself says, "A lot of people want to make me into gossip—and it's missing the point of anybody to make them into gossip."

Little Francis is a historical curiosity, but more besides. For all Carrington's authentic simplicity of manner, her text is rich in allusions to Surrealist works—the opening scene of *L'Age d'or*, when the bishops metamorphose into rocks, for instance—but also in imagery with roots elsewhere. In the story Leonora cast herself as a boy: the nephew of Uncle Ubriaco, whom he loves, and the rival for his affections with his fourteen-year-old daughter. The first scene shows Francis trying on an item from Uncle Ubriaco's collection, a purple and black corset, and finding that even laced tight it doesn't fit. Behind the oxymorons of typical Surrealist grotesquerie, one can discover the hankering of a young girl after the model woman of fantasy, who would fill the corset with her curves. Leonora still refers to herself as a *puer aeternus*, and Little Francis belongs, she says, in her inner world, as one of her several selves. By changing herself into a youth, she uncovered a deeper truth about her relation to Max Ernst, revealing in the devotion and passivity of the boy Francis the tutelage in which Ernst and other masters held their *femmes-enfants*, their brides of the wind; similarly, by transforming Ernst's wife into his daughter, Leonora unveiled that relation of dependence and authority as well.

Little Francis also inaugurates Leonora Carrington's lifelong exploration of the potential of the androgyne. When she wrote the novella, she had not yet read Jung, who was to influence her thought deeply later, but she had come across Mme. Alexandra David-Neel's works *With Mystics and Magicians in Tibet* and *Initiations and Initiates in Tibet* (both 1931), in which the eccentric traveler describes how, disguised as a man, she undertook a journey to illumination in the Himalayas. It is possible that the relations between Uncle Ubriaco and Little Francis, the nephew's unquestioning obedience to the older man in their adventures, spiritual and other, and the sexless character of the narrative relationship were influenced by the tales of Tibetan novices' spiritual struggle toward enlightenment in the custody of a lama. Androgyny betokens completeness, the union of male and female forces in a single individual, and a consequent blissful condition of desirelessness; sexual asceticism can be one of the methods used to uncover the yang forces within a woman. Many of Leonora's later paintings, however, as well as the novel *The Stone Door*, dramatize the attainment of this ideal by other means: Jung's *conjunctio oppositorum*, a man and a woman meeting in love.

Little Francis's masculinity does not communicate wholeness, only youth. His vulnerability remains deep. The change of sex also expresses Leonora's personal frustrations at being a girl; and not on account of some inner psychological inability to accept her femaleness. A spirited and intelligent young woman of her time and background was unbearably constrained by society. As her heroine protests in *The Stone Door*, "Little girls can't do the same things as little boys, they say. It isn't true. . . . I have three brothers. . . . They all do what they like because they are boys. It isn't fair. When I grow up I'll shave and put hair oil on my face to grow a beard. . . . I'm the only one that has to practise the piano for hours, wash all day, and say thank you for everything. You should see the clothes they make me wear." The well-known love of Englishwomen for horses may arise as much from the social freedom riding gives them as from a Lawrentian release of the libido. Leonora, on a horse, in riding gear, stripped herself of that encumbering femininity prescribed by her class and her family; when she left them behind to elope with Max Ernst, she first saw her herself as a boy and then gave herself a horse's head as well, rather like Joan of Arc when she left home—a rather different home—to fight as a knight for her king. Around the time she was writing *Little Francis*, Leonor Fini painted Leonora's portrait in armour, like an Amazon.

For the name of her hero, Leonora Carrington chose—unconsciously—that of the saint most famous for his affinity with all creatures, with "dear brother Donkey" and the birds to whom he preached. In the novella Little Francis indeed follows his namesake and eavesdrops on the conversation of creatures. A Carrington protagonist inhabits an animist world, in which hedgehogs warn of "the terrible imbecility of destiny" and even vegetables have souls (live sponges swim in the queen's bath in "The Royal Summons"); phenomena move at ease between categories—in *Little Francis*, "Miraldalocks" begins as a bewitched Goldilocks, the victim of a Gothic fairy tale who is turned into a plant resembling a mandrake root or marijuana; Uncle Ubriaco and Francis then pick it and smoke it; later still she materializes in person and enters the story of Little Francis's hallucinatory sufferings.

In the 1937 Paris exhibition at which Leonora first showed her paintings, the original sheets of Max Ernst's collage novel of 1934, *Une Semaine de bonté*, were also on display. *A Week of Kindness, or The Seven Capital Elements*, subjects a sweet-faced and imperturbable young heroine to floods and mayhem, fire and assault in a wickedly adroit parody of the penny-dreadful picture romance. This book and its earlier companions, *La Femme 100 têtes* (*The Hundred-Headed Woman*) and *Une Petite Fille rêve d'entrer au Carmel* (*A Little Girl Dreams of Taking the Veil*), mock the formulae of Ernst's Catholic boyhood—Passion Week, the love language of the Song of Songs, martyrdom stories. Leonora Carrington, faithful to the Surrealist love of blasphemy—where would the movement be without apostasy?—shapes Little Francis to the mould of her abandoned faith too, specifically to the Catholic Truth Society pamphlet on a saint's exemplary life. Her protagonist suffers numerous horrors; exactly like virgins who are put again and again to the torture and miraculously resist, remaining alive to undergo yet more, Little Francis watches himself guillotined and then survives, in horse form, to meet another gruesome fate.

The story proceeds through unholy encounters, like the banquet at Mâze, and ends in blasphemy, with a scene that Luis Buñuel might have filmed. Like Buñuel too, but unlike a lot of literary Surrealists, Leonora Carrington sustains throughout the peculiar transgressions she describes an inconsequent, dry tone and well-bred English manners. Throughout her writings, traditional ditties, songs, snatches of verse return, often ribald and irreverent, in the English upper class schoolboy style so admired by the Surrealists, who mostly came from a bourgeoisie that had never known such casual confidence in lawlessness and obscenity. The conscious source for her hero's name, for instance, was not Saint Francis of Assisi but a nursery rhyme of the variety of Harry Graham's *Ruthless Rhymes for Heartless Homes*:

> *Little Francis home from school*
> *Swung the baby by his tool:*
> *Mother screamed, Auntie shuddered,*
> *Father muttered, "I'll be buggered!"*
> *Nanny said, "Naughty Francis!*
> *You've ruined Baby's future chances."*

Leonora's background of nursery rituals and class privilege provided her with a heaped storehouse to raid: those first paintings, shown by André Breton in Paris in 1937 and in Amsterdam later the same year are now mislaid, but their titles disclose how she was plundering what was marvellous from the banalities of a propertied family's daily round: *Lord Candlestick's Meal*, *What Shall We Do Today, Aunt Amelia?* Because she broke with

England, joined the Surrealist movement in France, and has been identified with French Surrealism through her publishing history in various journals of the movement, it is easy to mistake Leonora for a foreign voice and overlook her closeness to a thoroughly Anglo-Saxon tradition on the one hand and to the Irish faery lore communicated by her mother on the other. Yet the stance she adopts often reminds the reader of one of Hilaire Belloc's wicked children, although she is telling stories from their point of view, not from the admonishing grown-ups' angle of the *Cautionary Tales*. She becomes Matilda, "who told lies and was Burned to Death," or Rebecca Offendort, who "was not really bad at heart, / But only rather rude and wild." She becomes Alice too, looking with Alice's eyes at Wonderland, though at the same time she continues to experience woman's doubled identity, feeling the eyes of others upon her, identifying with them as they comment on her looks and her demeanour and, as often as not, disapprove of her, like the father in "The Oval Lady," who orders the horse Tartar to be burned. As in Lewis Carroll's books, Leonora's stories present a world regulated by obscure commands and instructions, which the farouche heroine infringes by mistake or refuses on purpose. It becomes a contrary place, where she finds herself at odds, "born with a lacerated nature," as Jeremy tells Theodora in *The Baa Lambs' Holiday*.

In the spring of 1938, when Max Ernst finally separated from his wife and settled with Leonora in the hills near Saint-Martin, Ernst's sense of fantasy and play found her a willing accomplice. They decorated the small farmhouse together, Ernst sculpting magnificent tall bird- and fish-headed household gods and goddesses in cement on the exterior walls, Leonora making horses' heads and painting the walls and furniture. She was writing too, with inspiration, mainly short stories in an eccentric

French, for the benefit of Ernst (with whom she spoke French) and their friends. *La Maison de la peur* (*The House of Fear*) was the first to be published, in 1938, with its original spelling and grammar intact (Ernst's "beautiful language, truthful and pure"), with collage illustrations by Ernst; a second collection, *La Dame Ovale* (*The Oval Lady*), followed the year after. It included "The Debutante," "A Man in Love," "The Royal Summons," and "Uncle Sam Carrington," again with mock-solemn illustrations by Ernst. Many of the stories in *The Seventh Horse and Other Tales*, being published simultaneously with this volume, were tapped out on an old portable machine in the house in Saint-Martin at this time. In these stories Leonora Carrington achieves a rare tone, at once naïve and perverse, comic and lethal.

She acknowledges that Ernst was a uniquely inspiring companion, with whom she discovered a new way of living; he could turn everything into play—cooking, keeping house, gardening. Shapshots of those days show the artist Leonor Fini in fancy dress, friends from England and Paris in drag, Leonora herself in lace and bell-fringed shawls chosen by Fini; memoirs tell of excursions, general high spirits, practical jokes. (Leonora's were often culinary: she might cook an omelet with hair cut from the head of a guest while he slept and serve it to him, or dye sago black by cooking it in squid's ink and dish it up with cracked ice and lemon as caviare for a collector paying a call.) Although temperamentally she resists reminiscing, she says of this time, just before the war, "It was an era of paradise."

In 1939, after the French declared war on Germany, Max Ernst was arrested as an enemy alien and sent to a camp. Leonora followed him, supplying him with paints and other materials and lobbying for his release. Ernst was in double danger, for he was undesirable to the Germans too; his painting *La Belle Jardinière* had toured the country in the Nazis' show of "Degenerate Art."

Leonora went to Paris and managed to get him released, and Ernst returned from the camp at Largentière to Saint-Martin. Then early the following year, after the Germans crossed the Maginot Line, Ernst was arrested again and put in a camp farther away, at Les Milles near Aix, with hundreds of other aliens (including Hans Bellmer, who painted his portrait there). Leonora, left alone in Saint-Martin, travelled to Paris to sue for his freedom, but she found the shut doors of cowardice and silence everywhere; France was falling. She returned to Saint-Martin and began to suffer the madness she describes in *Down Below*.

Down Below gives an exceptionally clear and detailed account of the experience of going insane. As a text, it derives its peculiar flavour from this antinomy at its heart, that it is a narrative, apparently rationally composed and lucidly recalled, about recent, hair-raisingly unhinged behaviour. André Breton encouraged Leonora to write it; from his point of view, Leonora Carrington, wild muse, *femme-enfant*, had realised one of the most desirable ambitions of Surrealism, the voyage down into madness. In the preface to Max Ernst's *Hundred Headless Woman*, Breton had spoken of "our will to absolute disorientation." Leonora had found it. She was Nadja *retrouvée*, the heroine of Breton's text returned to "normal," an instrument of *l'amour fou* and its victim. She had truly experienced the dementia Breton and Paul Éluard had only been able to simulate in *L'Immaculée Conception* of 1930, though their impersonation of insanity later won Jacques Lacan's applause.

Down Below has had a complicated history: Leonora first wrote a short version in English and showed it to Janet Flanner, who was then working in a New York publishing house; she wasn't interested. The text was subsequently lost during Leonora's move from New York to Mexico; however, Pierre Mabille, a surgeon and an intimate of the Surrealist circle in France, urged her to reconstruct it. The text, as it now stands, is addressed to him and was begun by Leonora in August 1943, on the third anniversary of the events she recalls, in the abandoned Russian Embassy in Mexico City, where she, Mabille, and other refugees were camping. Leonora then talked it through in French to Jeanne Megnen, Mabille's wife, who established the first published version in French. This was then translated back into English by Victor Llona for the Surrealist journal *VVV*, which was edited in New York by David Hare and, for a period, Marcel Duchamp. *Down Below* came out in the issue of February 1944, soon after the short story "The Seventh Horse" (the title story of the accompanying volume of short stories now published), almost two years before Henri Parisot was able to publish it in France, where it appeared in the collection *L'Age d'or* immediately after the war.

This journey to and from oral and written versions, to and from French and English translations, accounts for the difference in tone between *Down Below* and Leonora's other writings. As a testament to the horrors of psychosis, as evidence of medical treatment and convulsive drug therapy, *Down Below* ranks beside autobiographical fiction like Antonia White's *The Sugar House*, Sylvia Plath's *The Bell Jar*, and Janet Frame's *Faces in the Water*, but it has only moments of distinctive Carrington drollness. It's as if, in her dementia, she vacated her own being, becoming for a while other, uttering in a different voice, to a different pace, using another sentence structure. Leonora herself, who has since studied Tibetan Buddhism, does not adhere to a classical Western notion of the fixed self and considers the person of *Down Below* another member of her disparate inner population. On a literary level, however, *Down Below* belongs more closely to the genre of autobiographical record advocated by Breton and practised by him in both *Nadja* and *L'Amour fou*; tracing off daily experience, the writer-seeker uncovers marvellous patternings brought about by *le hasard objectif* (objective chance) and reaches illumination. In its pitilessness too (though it can provoke pity, *Down Below* shows none), the work reflects Surrealism's cult of madness, especially female madness, as another conductor to the invisible world.

Leonora's descent into madness consecrated her as a Surrealist heroine, regardless of the cost to her of her sufferings. She talks of the "Terror" she felt and still feels, and though she has not had to contend again with anything like the prolonged bout of insanity described in *Down Below*, the experience marked her in ways that were not altogether *"merveilleux."* The "breakthrough" achieved by the *"dérèglement de tous les sens"* sought by Rimbaud and his successors can hardly be recommended, and *Down Below* tacitly reflects this ambivalence. "After the experience of *Down Below*, I changed. Dramatically. It was very much like having been dead," she says now. "It was very clear, I was possessed. I'd suffered so much when Max was taken away to the camp, I entered a catatonic state, and I was no longer suffering in an ordinary human dimension. I was in another place, it was something quite different. Quite different."

Magouche Fielding, who was married to Arshile Gorky in New York in the forties when the Surrealists gathered there, says drily, "Surrealism wasn't good for your health. I don't think anyone would take it as a cure. It was like filleting fish, taking out the backbone of quite ordinary people. Max Ernst, now, was as strong as an ox."

In the postscript appended here to the 1943 version of *Down Below*, Leonora Carrington tells the story of her escape from her minder in Lisbon and her meeting there by chance with Ernst. He was now with Peggy Guggenheim, who was helping him reach America. It was a time of great anguish for all of them: in Lisbon Leonora had married Renato Leduc, a Mexican diplomat and bullfighting aficionado whom she had first met with

Picasso in Paris. But, as Peggy Guggenheim recounted in her memoirs, Ernst and Leonora, though separated by circumstances, still shared a deep inner bond of fantasy, feeling, and experience.

With many other refugees from a vanquished France, they arrived in New York in 1941, by different routes; in spite of all the upheavals, it was a time of inspired work for both of them. Leonora's painting was changing. Before her spell in the asylum, she had seen Bosch's paintings in the Prado. Their influence was profound, as anyone who knows her art may judge. During the war she developed the intricately visionary style of her mature work, peopling her panels with dreamscapes, imaginary beings, smoking volcanoes, ice floes. She made a portrait of Max Ernst, in which he wears stripy socks in the colours Uncle Ubriaco used on Little Francis's coffin. The small painting seems to offer a reply to Ernst's grandiloquent work *The Robing of the Bride* of 1940; the red feathers of his mermaid's tail cloak echo the scarlet feathered robe of the bride herself. In the Carrington painting, the white unicorn, her animal familiar, appears twice, frozen in the icy landscape and again, trapped in the glass lantern Ernst holds in his hand. Ernst gave her a portrait in turn, *Leonora in the Morning Light*, showing her rising out of an Ernst jungle, parting its tentacular growth; he also painted during this period *The Spanish Physician*, an eloquent vision of the desperation of *Down Below*.

Leonora Carrington today resists commenting on the connection between the two artists in their symbols; it was eerie to be with her in the Metropolitan Museum in New York in 1987 as she passed by, without comment, another Ernst painting of 1940, *Napoleon in the Desert*, in which he portrayed himself, horse-headed, in exile on the same rocky outcrop as the beautiful ripe Bride, who holds herself at a distance, unmoved by his presence. Incomparably original in old age as in youth,

Leonora Carrington does not dwell on the past but renews herself at every stage without either the nostalgia or the disavowals so common in retrospection.

In 1942 Leonora Carrington left New York for Mexico, where many Surrealists were settling, including Benjamin Péret, the poet, and his wife, the artist Remedios Varo, who were to become intimate friends of Leonora's. Renato Leduc was now working as a bullfighting correspondent, and they soon parted, amicably; Leonora married Cziki Weisz, a Hungarian photographer who had run Robert Capa's outfit in Paris. She had two sons, Gabriel and Pablo: the experience of motherhood inspired some of her most delicate and glowing paintings, *L'amor che move 'l sole e le altre stelle*, *Tuesday*, *Palatine Predella*, and later *We Saw the Daughter of the Minotaur*. She continued to write stories, drama, and her first novel, *The Stone Door*, about her marriage to Weisz. She adapted "The Oval Lady," in *Penelope*, a stage play in 1946; it ends on a new note of savage optimism, with the heroine's escape on Tartar's back and the suicide of her repressive father. In *The Hearing Trumpet*, a novel published in English in 1976, she sustained her unique blend of enigma and comedy, enlightenment alongside farce, over a greater length than in any fiction she had written before.

Widely read in alchemical writings, a regular pilgrim since 1971 to the lamas in exile from Tibet, analysed by followers of Jung, and loyal to a fierce and personal brand of feminist idealism, Leonora Carrington never altogether sheds in her quest for wisdom a wonderful, saving mischievousness.

Her great friend and collector Edward James wrote over her door in Mexico, "This is the house of the Sphinx." A sphinx, yes, but a sphinx who sets riddles not to confound or mock but to provoke laughter and open doors in the chambers of the mind, where love and fear and the other passions have their seat. She has said,

"I try to empty myself of images which have made me blind": in many ways she is breaking spells which blind others' sight too, although the landscape she travels remains a place enchanted.

> MARINA WARNER
> *Kentish Town—Santa Monica, 1987*

My thanks, above all, to Leonora Carrington, for her time and her company. I would like also to acknowledge the inspiration of Whitney Chadwick and her book *Women Artists and the Surrealist Movement* (London, 1986), which introduced me to Leonora Carrington; the help of Janice Helland, and of her thesis, "Daughter of the Minotaur: Leonora Carrington and the Surrealist Image" (University of Victoria, British Columbia, 1984); the transcript of a radio interview Leonora Carrington gave Germaine Rouvre in 1977; and Gloria Orenstein's unpublished paper "Hermeticism and Surrealism in the Visual Works of Leonora Carrington" (1982).

THE HOUSE OF FEAR

She looked slightly like a horse . . .

Preface, or Loplop Presents the Bride of the Wind

On the threshold of a house of imposing size, the only house in a town built of thunderbolt stone, two nightingales hold each other tightly entwined. The silence of the sun presides over their frolic. The sun strips off its black skirt and white bodice. And is gone. Night falls at a stroke, with a crash.

Behold this man: in water up to his knees, he stands proudly upright. Violent caresses have left luminous traces on his superb pearly body. What on earth is he doing, this man with his turquoise gaze, his lips flushed with generous desires? This man is bringing joy to the landscape.

What on earth is this white cloud doing? This white cloud escapes hissing, from a spilt basket. It is bringing life to nature.

Where have these two strange people sprung from, coming slowly down the street, followed by a thousand dwarfs? Is this the man they call Loplop, the Bird Superior, because of his gentle, fierce character? On his huge white hat he has caught in midflight an extraordinary bird with emerald plumage, a hooked beak, and a hard look. He has no fear. He has come from the house of fear. And the woman, whose upper arm is encircled by a narrow thread of blood, must be none other than the Bride of the Wind.

Horses in all the windows. "Good morning, cousin. Good morning, cousin. What good wind has brought you hither?"

Good wind, ill wind, I present to you the Bride of the Wind.

Who is the Bride of the Wind? Can she read? Can she write French without mistakes? What wood does she burn to keep warm?

She warms herself with her intense life, her mystery, her poetry. She has read nothing, but drunk everything. She can't read. And yet the nightingale saw her, sitting on the stone of spring, reading. And though she was reading to herself, the animals and horses listened to her in admiration.

For she was reading *The House of Fear*, this true story you are now going to read, this story written in a beautiful language, truthful and pure.

MAX ERNST
1938

The House of Fear

One day towards half past midday, as I was walking in a certain neighborhood, I met a horse who stopped me.

"Come with me," he said, bending his head towards a street that was dark and narrow. "I've something I particularly want to show you."

"I haven't the time," I replied, but nevertheless I followed him. We came to a door on which he knocked with his left hoof. The door opened. We went in, I thought I'd be late for lunch.

There were a number of creatures in ecclesiastical dress. "Do go upstairs," they told me. "There you'll see our beautiful inlaid floor. It is completely made of turquoise, and the tiles are stuck together with gold."

Surprised by such a welcome, I nodded my head and made a sign to the horse to show me this treasure. The staircase had enormously high steps, but we went up without difficulty, the horse and I.

"You know, it isn't really as beautiful as all that," he told me in a low voice. "But one's got to make a living, hasn't one?"

All of a sudden we saw the turquoise paving which covered the floor of a large, empty room. In fact the tiles were well fitted together with gold, and the blue was dazzling. I gazed at it politely, the horse thoughtfully:

"Well, you see, I'm really bored by this job. I only do it for the money. I don't really belong in these surroundings. I'll show you, next time there's a party."

After due reflection, I said to myself that it was easy to see that this horse wasn't just an ordinary horse. Having reached this conclusion, I felt I should get to know him better.

"I'll certainly come to your party. I'm beginning to think I rather like you."

"You yourself are an improvement on the usual run of customers," he replied. "I'm very good at telling the difference between ordinary people and those with a certain understanding. I've got the gift of immediately getting right inside a person's soul."

I smiled anxiously. "And when is the party?"

"It's this evening. Put on some warm clothes."

That was odd, for outside the sun was shining brightly.

Going down the stairs at the far end of the room, I noticed with surprise that the horse managed much better than I. The ecclesiastics had disappeared, and I left without anyone seeing me go.

"At nine o'clock," the horse said. "I'll call for you at nine. Be sure to let the concierge know."

On my way home I thought to myself that I ought to have asked the horse to dinner.

Never mind, I thought. I bought some lettuce and some potatoes for my supper. When I got home I lit a

I noticed with surprise that the horse...

little fire to prepare my meal. I had a cup of tea, thought about my day and mostly about the horse whom, though I'd only known him a short time, I called my friend. I have few friends and am glad to have a horse for a friend. After the meal I smoked a cigarette and mused on the luxury it would be to go out, instead of talking to myself and boring myself to death with the same endless stories I'm forever telling myself. I am a very boring person, despite my enormous intelligence and distinguished appearance, and nobody knows this better than I. I've often told myself that if only I were given the opportunity, I'd perhaps become the centre of intellectual society. But by dint of talking to myself so much, I tend to repeat the same things all the time. But what can you expect? I'm a recluse.

It was in the course of these reflections that my friend the horse knocked on my door, with such force that I was afraid the neighbours would complain.

"I'm coming," I called out.

In the darkness I didn't see which direction we were taking. I ran beside him, clinging to his mane for support. Soon I noticed that in front of us, behind us, and on all sides in the open country were more and more horses. They were staring straight ahead and each carried some green stuff in its mouth. They were hurrying, the noise of their hooves shook the earth. The cold became intense.

"This party takes place every year," the horse said.

"It doesn't look as if they were enjoying themselves much," I said.

"We're visiting the Castle of Fear. She's the mistress of the house."

The castle stood ahead of us, and he explained that it was built of stones that held the cold of winter.

"Inside it's even colder," he said, and when we got into the courtyard I realised that he was telling the truth. The horses all shivered, and their teeth chattered like castanets. I had the impression that all the horses in the world had come to this party. Each one with bulging eyes, fixed straight ahead, and each one with foam frozen around its lips. I didn't dare speak, I was too terrified.

Following one another in single file, we reached a great hall decorated with mushrooms and other fruits of the night. The horses all sat down on their hindquarters, their forelegs rigid. They looked about without moving their heads, just showing the whites of their eyes. I was very much afraid. In front of us, reclining in the Roman fashion on a very large bed, lay the mistress of the house—Fear. She looked slightly like a horse, but was much uglier. Her dressing gown was made of live bats sewn together by their wings: the way they fluttered, one would have thought they didn't much like it.

"My friends," she said, weeping and trembling. "For three hundred and sixty-five days I've been thinking of the best way to entertain you this night. Supper will be as usual, and everyone is entitled to three portions. But apart from that I have thought up a new game which I think is particularly original, for I've spent a lot of time perfecting it. I hope with all my heart that all of you will experience the same joy in playing this game as I have found in devising it."

A deep silence followed her words. Then she continued.

"I shall now give you all the details. I shall supervise the game myself, and I shall be the umpire and decide who wins.

"You must all count backwards from a hundred and ten to five as quickly as possible while thinking of your own fate and weeping for those who have gone before you. You must simultaneously beat time to the tune of 'the Volga Boatmen' with your left foreleg, 'The Marseillaise' with your right foreleg, and 'Where Have You Gone, My Last Rose of Summer?' with your two back legs. I had some further details, but I've left them out to simplify the game. Now let us begin. And don't forget that, though I can't see all over the hall at once, the Good Lord sees everything."

I don't know whether it was the terrible cold that excited such enthusiasm, the fact is that the horses began to beat the floor with their hooves as if they wanted to descend to the depths of the earth. I stayed where I was, hoping she wouldn't see me, but I had an uncomfortable feeling that she could see me very well with her great eye (she had only one eye, but it was six times bigger than an ordinary eye). It went on like this for twenty-five minutes, but . . .

but...

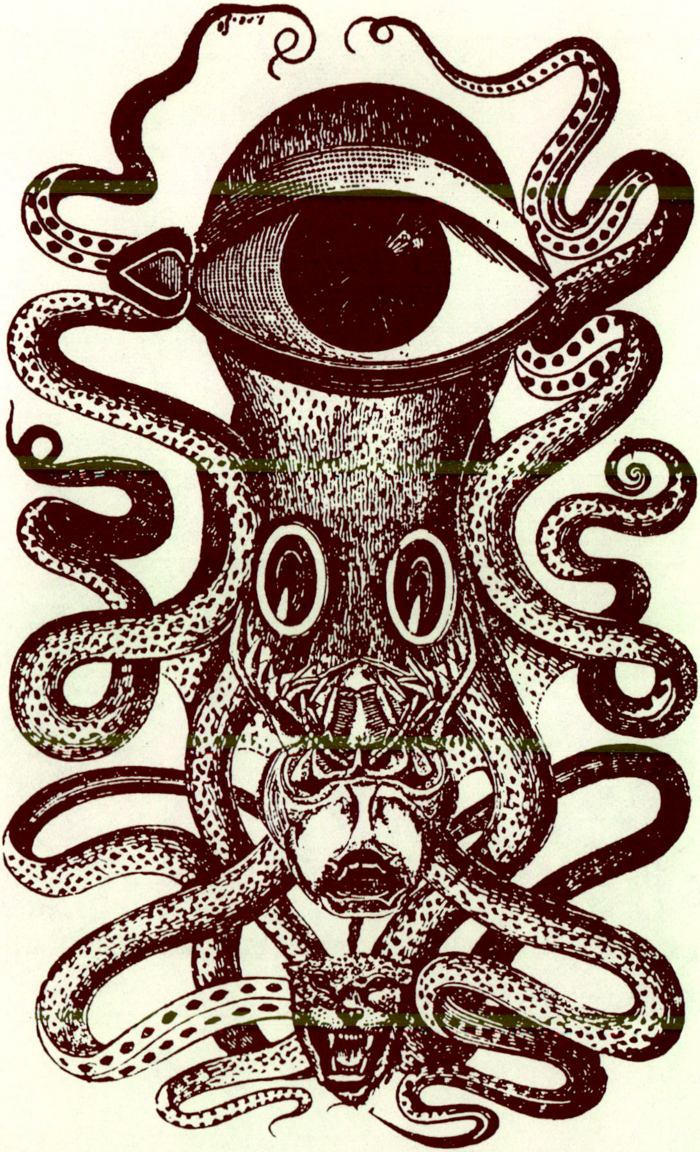

THE OVAL LADY

The Oval Lady

A very tall thin lady was standing at the window. The window was very high and very thin too. The lady's face was pale and sad. She didn't move, and nothing moved in the window except the pheasant feather in her hair. My eyes kept being drawn to the quivering feather: it was so restless in the window, where nothing was moving!

This was the seventh time I had passed in front of this window. The sad lady hadn't stirred; in spite of the cold that evening, I stopped. Perhaps the furniture in the room was as long and thin as the lady and the window. Perhaps the cat, if there were a cat, would also conform to their elegant proportions. I wanted to know, I was devoured by curiosity, an irresistible desire took hold of me to enter the house, simply to find out.

Before I knew exactly what I was doing, I had reached the entrance hall. The door closed quietly behind me, and for the first time in my life I found myself inside a stately home. It was overwhelming. For a start, there was such a distinguished silence that I hardly dared to breathe. Then there was the incredible elegance of the furniture and the trinkets. Every chair was at least twice as tall as an ordinary chair, and very much narrower. For these aristocrats, even plates were oval, not round like ordinary people's. The drawing room, where the sad lady was standing, was adorned with a fireplace, and there was a table laid with teacups and cakes. Near the fire, a teapot waited quietly to be poured.

Seen from the back, the lady seemed even taller. She was at least ten feet tall. The problem was how to speak to her. Begin with the weather, and how bad it was? Too banal. Talk of poetry? But what poetry?

"Madam, do you like poetry?"

"No, I hate poetry," she answered in a voice stifled with boredom, without turning to me.

"Have a cup of tea, it will make you feel better."

"I don't drink, I don't eat. It's a protest against my father, the bastard."

After a quarter of an hour's silence she turned around, and I was astonished by her youth. She was perhaps sixteen years old.

"You're very tall for your age, Miss. When I was sixteen I wasn't half as tall as you."

"I don't care. Anyway, give me some tea, but don't tell anyone. Perhaps I'll also have one of those cakes, but whatever you do, remember not to say anything."

She ate with an absolutely amazing appetite. When she got to the twentieth cake she said, "Even if I die of hunger, he'll never win. I can see the funeral procession now, with four big black horses, gleaming. They're walking slowly, my little coffin, white in a drift of red roses. And people weeping, weeping. . . ."

She began to weep.

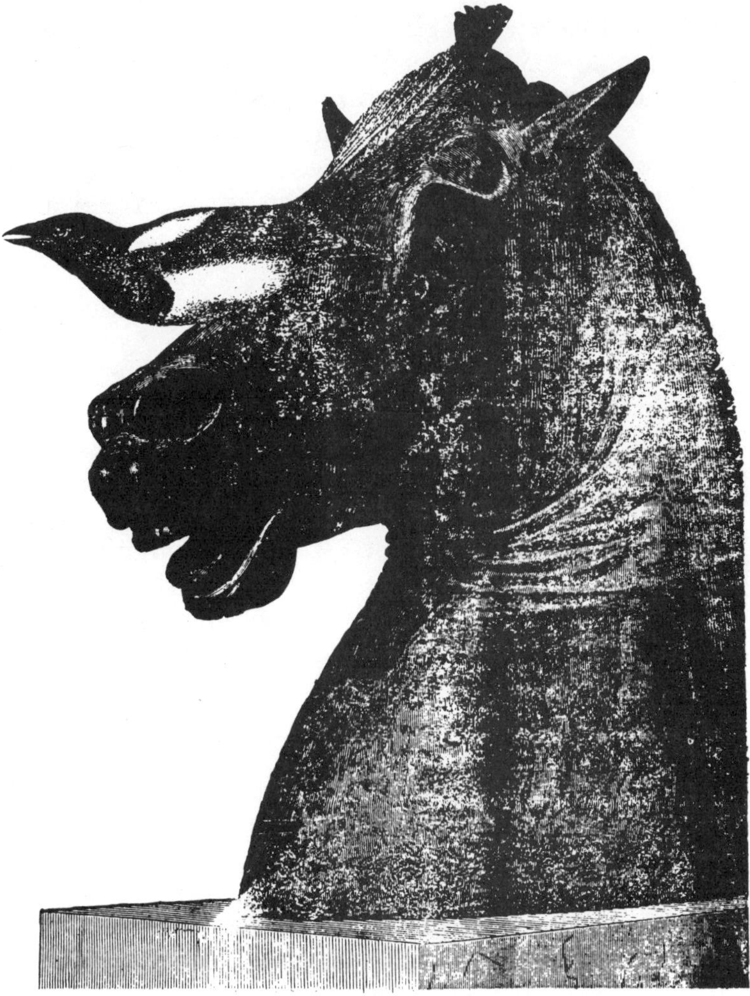

"Look at the little corpse of beautiful Lucretia. And you know, once you're dead, there's nothing very much one can do. I'd like to starve myself to death just to annoy him. What a pig."

With these words she slowly left the room. I followed her.

When we reached the third floor, we went into an enormous nursery where hundreds of dilapidated and broken toys lay all over the place. Lucretia went up to a wooden horse. In spite of its great age—certainly not much less than a hundred years—it was frozen in a gallop.

"Tartar is my favourite," she said, stroking the horse's muzzle. "He loathes my father."

Tartar rocked himself gracefully on his rockers, and I wondered to myself how he could move by himself. Lucretia looked at him thoughtfully, clasping her hands together.

"He'll travel a very long way like that," she said. "And when he comes back he'll tell me something interesting."

Looking out of doors, I noticed that it was snowing. It was very cold, but Lucretia didn't notice it. A slight sound at the window attracted her attention.

"It's Matilda," she said. "I ought to have left the window open. Anyway, it's stifling in here." With that she broke the windowpanes, and in came the snow with a magpie, which flew around the room three times.

"Matilda talks like this. It's ten years since I split her tongue in two. What a beautiful creature."

"Beautiful crrrreature," screeched Matilda in a witch's voice. "Beeeautiful crrrreature."

Matilda went and perched on Tartar's head. The horse was still galloping gently. He was covered in snow.

"Did you come to play with us?" enquired Lucretia. "I'm glad, because I get very bored here. Let's make believe that we're all horses. I'll turn myself into a horse;

with some snow, it'll be more convincing. You be a horse too, Matilda."

"Horse, horse, horse," yelled Matilda, dancing hysterically on Tartar's head. Lucretia threw herself into the snow, which was already deep, and rolled in it, shouting, "We are all horses!"

When she emerged, the effect was extraordinary. If I hadn't known that it was Lucretia, I would have sworn that it was a horse. She was beautiful, a blinding white all over, with four legs as fine as needles, and a mane which fell around her long face like water. She laughed with joy and danced madly around in the snow.

"Gallop, gallop, Tartar, but I shall go faster than you."

Tartar didn't change speed, but his eyes sparkled. One could only see his eyes, for he was covered in snow. Matilda cawed and struck her head against the walls. As for me, I danced a sort of polka so as not to die of cold.

Suddenly I noticed that the door was open, and that an old woman stood framed in the doorway. She had been there perhaps for a long time without my noticing her. She looked at Lucretia with a nasty stare.

"Stop at once," she cried, suddenly trembling with fury. "What's all this? Eh, my young ladies? Lucretia, you know this game has been strictly forbidden by your father. This ridiculous game. You aren't a child anymore."

Lucretia danced on, flinging out her four legs dangerously near the old woman; her laughter was piercing.

"Stop, Lucretia!"

Lucretia's voice became more and more shrill. She was doubled up with laughter.

"All right," said the old woman. "So you won't obey me, young lady? All right, you'll regret it. I'm going to take you to your father."

One of her hands was hidden behind her back, but with astonishing speed for someone so old, she jumped on Lucretia's back and forced a bit between her teeth.

Lucretia leapt into the air, neighing with rage, but the old woman held on. After that she caught each of us, me by my hair and Matilda by her head, and all four of us were hurled into a frenzied dance. In the corridor, Lucretia kicked out everywhere and smashed pictures and chairs and china. The old woman clung to her back like a limpet to a rock. I was covered in cuts and bruises, and thought Matilda must be dead, for she was fluttering sadly in the old woman's hand like a rag.

We arrived in the dining room in a veritable orgy of noise. Sitting at the end of a long table an old gentleman, looking more like a geometric figure than anything else, was finishing his meal. All at once complete silence fell in the room. Lucretia looked at her father with swollen eyes.

"So you're starting up your old tricks again," he said, cracking a hazelnut. "Mademoiselle de la Rochefroide did well to bring you here. It's exactly three years and three days since I forbade you to play at horses. This is the seventh time that I have had to punish you, and you are no doubt aware that in our family, seven is the last number. I'm afraid, my dear Lucretia, that this time I shall have to punish you pretty severely."

The girl, who had taken the appearance of a horse, did not move, but her nostrils quivered.

"What I'm going to do is purely for your own good, my dear." His voice was very gentle. "You're too old to play with Tartar. Tartar is for children. I am going to burn him myself, until there's nothing left of him."

Lucretia gave a terrible cry and fell to her knees.

"Not that, Papa, not that."

The old man smiled with great sweetness and cracked another hazelnut.

"It's the seventh time, my dear."

The tears ran from Lucretia's great horse's eyes and carved two channels in her cheeks of snow. She turned such a dazzling white that she shone like a star.

"Have pity, Papa, have pity. Don't burn Tartar."

Her shrill voice grew thinner and thinner, and she was soon kneeling in a pool of water. I was afraid that she was going to melt away.

"Mademoiselle de la Rochefroide, take Miss Lucretia outside," said her father, and the old woman took the poor creature, who had become all thin and trembling, out of the room.

I don't think he had noticed I was there. I hid behind the door and heard the old man go up to the nursery. A little later I stopped my ears with my fingers, for the most frightful neighing sounded from above, as if an animal were suffering extreme torture.

The Debutante

When I was a debutante, I often went to the zoo. I went so often that I knew the animals better than I knew girls of my own age. Indeed it was in order to get away from people that I found myself at the zoo every day. The animal I got to know best was a young hyena. She knew me too. She was very intelligent. I taught her French, and she, in return, taught me her language. In this way we passed many pleasant hours.

My mother was arranging a ball in my honour on the first of May. During this time I was in a state of great distress for whole nights. I've always detested balls, especially when they are given in my honour.

On the morning of the first of May 1934, very early, I went to visit the hyena.

"What a bloody nuisance," I said to her. "I've got to go to my ball tonight."

"You're very lucky," she said. "I'd love to go. I don't know how to dance, but at least I could make small talk."

"There'll be a great many different things to eat," I told her. "I've seen truckloads of food delivered to our house."

"And you're complaining," replied the hyena, disgusted. "Just think of me, I eat once a day, and you can't imagine what a heap of bloody rubbish I'm given."

I had an audacious idea, and I almost laughed. "All you have to do is to go instead of me!"

"We don't resemble each other enough, otherwise I'd gladly go," said the hyena rather sadly.

"Listen," I said. "No one sees too well in the evening light. If you disguise yourself, nobody will notice you in the crowd. Besides, we're practically the same size. You're my only friend, I beg you to do this for me."

She thought this over, and I knew that she really wanted to accept.

"Done," she said all of a sudden.

There weren't many keepers about, it was so early in the morning. I opened the cage quickly, and in a very few moments we were out in the street. I hailed a taxi; at home, everybody was still in bed. In my room I brought out the dress I was to wear that evening. It was a little long, and the hyena found it difficult to walk in my high-heeled shoes. I found some gloves to hide her hands, which were too hairy to look like mine. By the time the sun was shining into my room, she was able to make her way around the room several times, walking more or less upright. We were so busy that my mother almost opened the door to say good morning before the hyena had hidden under my bed.

"There's a bad smell in your room," my mother said, opening the window. "You must have a scented bath before tonight, with my new bath salts."

"Certainly," I said.

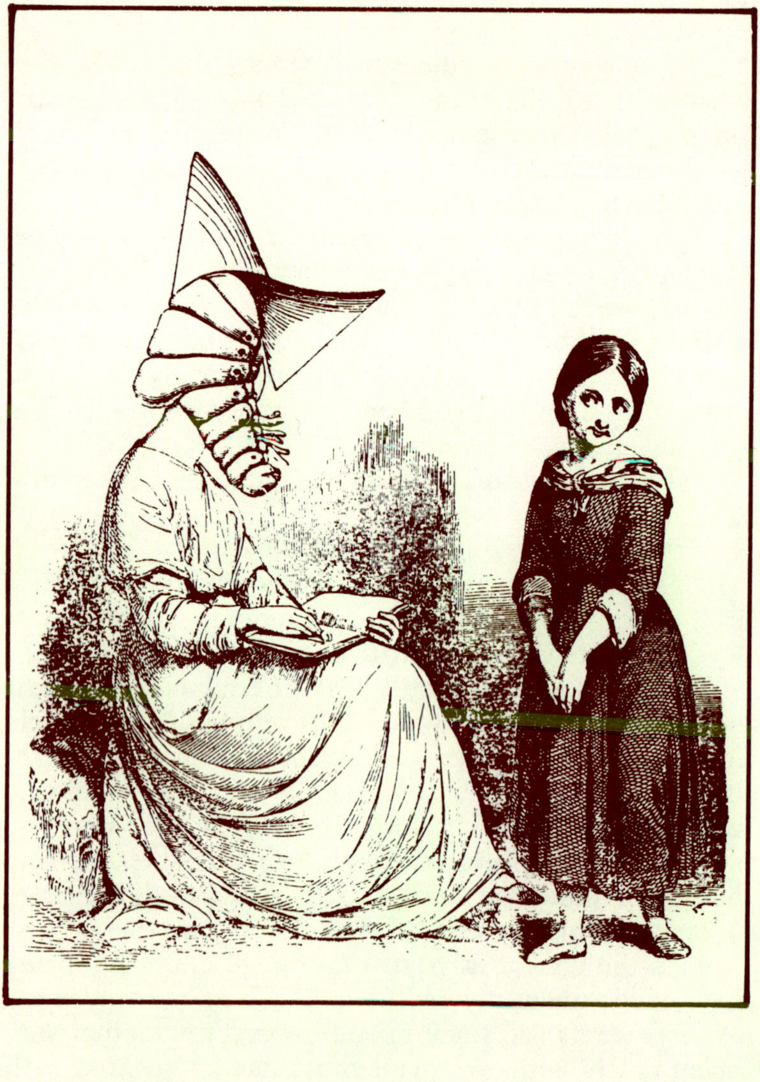

She didn't stay long. I think the smell was too much for her.

"Don't be late for breakfast," she said and left the room.

The greatest difficulty was to find a way of disguising the hyena's face. We spent hours and hours looking for a way, but she always rejected my suggestions. At last she said, "I think I've found the answer. Have you got a maid?"

"Yes," I said, puzzled.

"There you are then. Ring for your maid, and when she comes in we'll pounce upon her and tear off her face. I'll wear her face tonight instead of mine."

"It's not practical," I said. "She'll probably die if she hasn't got a face. Somebody will certainly find the corpse, and we'll be put in prison."

"I'm hungry enough to eat her," the hyena replied.

"And the bones?"

"As well," she said. "So, it's on?"

"Only if you promise to kill her before tearing off her face. It'll hurt her too much otherwise."

"All right. It's all the same to me."

Not without a certain amount of nervousness I rang for Mary, my maid. I certainly wouldn't have done it if I didn't hate having to go to a ball so much. When Mary came in I turned to the wall so as not to see. I must admit it didn't take long. A brief cry, and it was over. While the hyena was eating, I looked out the window. A few minutes later she said, "I can't eat any more. Her two feet are left over still, but if you have a little bag, I'll eat them later in the day."

"You'll find a bag embroidered with fleurs-de-lis in the cupboard. Empty out the handkerchiefs you'll find inside, and take it." She did as I suggested. Then she said, "Turn round now and look how beautiful I am."

In front of the mirror, the hyena was admiring herself in Mary's face. She had nibbled very neatly all around the face so that what was left was exactly what was needed.

"You've certainly done that very well," I said.

Towards evening, when the hyena was all dressed up, she declared, "I really feel in tip-top form. I have a feeling that I shall be a great success this evening."

When we had heard the music from downstairs for quite some time, I said to her, "Go on down now, and remember, don't stand next to my mother. She's bound to realise that it isn't me. Apart from her I don't know anybody. Best of luck." I kissed her as I left her, but she did smell very strong.

Night fell. Tired by the day's emotions, I took a book and sat down by the open window, giving myself up to peace and quiet. I remember that I was reading *Gulliver's Travels* by Jonathan Swift. About an hour later, I noticed the first signs of trouble. A bat flew in at the window, uttering little cries. I am terribly afraid of bats. I hid behind a chair, my teeth chattering. I had hardly gone down on my knees when the sound of beating wings was overcome by a great noise at my door. My mother entered, pale with rage.

"We'd just sat down at table," she said, "when that thing sitting in your place got up and shouted, 'So I smell a bit strong, what? Well, I don't eat cakes!' Whereupon it tore off its face and ate it. And with one great bound, disappeared through the window."

The Royal Summons

I had received a royal summons to pay a call on the sovereigns of my country.

The invitation was made of lace, framing embossed letters of gold. There were also roses and swallows.

I went to fetch my car, but my chauffeur, who has no practical sense at all, had just buried it.

"I did it to grow mushrooms," he told me. "There's no better way of growing mushrooms."

"Brady," I said to him, "you're a complete idiot. You have ruined my car."

So, since my car was indeed completely out of action, I was obliged to hire a horse and cart.

When I arrived at the palace, I was told by an impassive servant, dressed in red and gold, "The queen went mad yesterday. She's in her bath."

"How terrible," I exclaimed. "How did it happen?"

"It's the heat."

"May I see her all the same?" I didn't like the idea of my long journey being wasted.

"Yes," the servant replied. "You may see her anyway."

We passed down corridors decorated in imitation marble, admirably done, through rooms with Greek bas-reliefs and Medici ceilings and wax fruit everywhere.

The queen was in her bath when I went in; I noticed that she was bathing in goat's milk.

"Come on in," she said. "You see I use only live sponges. It's healthier."

The sponges were swimming about all over the place in the milk, and she had trouble catching them. A servant, armed with long-handled tongs, helped her from time to time.

"I'll soon be through with my bath," the Queen said. "I have a proposal to put to you. I would like you to see the government instead of me today, I'm too tired myself. They're all idiots, so you won't find it difficult."

"All right," I said.

The government chamber was at the other end of the palace. The ministers were sitting at a long and very shiny table.

As the representative of the Queen, I sat in the seat at the end. The Prime Minister rose and struck the table with a gavel. The table broke in two. Some servants came in with another table. The Prime Minister swapped the first gavel for another, made of rubber. He struck the table again and began to speak. "Madam Deputy of the Queen, ministers, friends. Our dearly beloved sovereign went mad yesterday, and so we need another. But first we must assassinate the old queen."

The ministers murmured amongst themselves for a while. Presently, the oldest minister rose to his feet and addressed the assembly. "That being the case, we must forthwith make a plan. Not only must we make a plan,

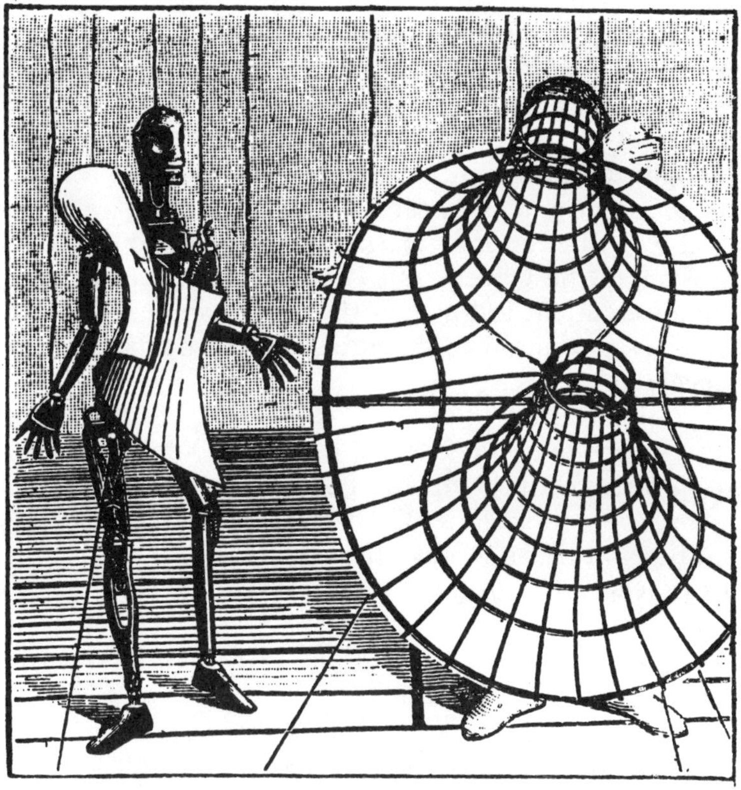

but we must come to a decision. We must choose who is to be the assassin."

All hands were immediately raised. I didn't quite know what to do as the deputy of Her Majesty.

Perplexed, the Prime Minister looked over the company.

"We can't all do it," he said. "But I've a very good idea. We'll play a game of draughts, and the winner has the right to assassinate the queen." He turned to me and asked, "Do you play Miss?"

I was filled with embarrassment. I had no desire to assassinate the Queen, and I foresaw that serious consequences might follow. On the other hand I had never been any good at all at draughts. So I saw no danger, and I accepted.

"I don't mind," I said.

"So, it's understood," said the Prime Minister. "This is what the winner will do: take the queen for a stroll in the Royal Menagerie. When you reach the lions (second cage on the left), push her in. I shall tell the keeper not to feed the lions until tomorrow."

The Queen called me to her office. She was watering the flowers woven in the carpet.

"Well, did it go all right?" she asked.

"Yes, it went very well," I answered, confused.

"Would you like some soup?"

"You're too kind," I said.

"It's mock beef tea. I make it myself," the Queen said. "There's nothing in it but potatoes."

While we were eating the broth, an orchestra played popular and classical tunes. The Queen loved music to distraction.

The meal over, the Queen left to have a rest. I for my part went to join in the game of draughts on the terrace. I was nervous, but I've inherited sporting instincts from my father. I had given my word to be there, and so there I would be.

The enormous terrace looked impressive. In front of the garden, darkened by the twilight and the cypress trees, the ministers were assembled. There were twenty little tables. Each had two chairs, with thin, fragile legs. When he saw me arrive, the Prime Minister called out, "Take your places," and everybody rushed to the tables and began to play ferociously.

We played all night without stopping. The only sounds that interrupted the game were an occasional furious bellow from one minister or another. Towards dawn, the blast of a trumpet abruptly called an end to the game. A voice, coming from I don't know where, cried, "She has won. She's the only person who didn't cheat."

I was rooted to the ground with horror.

"Who? Me?" I said.

"Yes, you," the voice replied, and I noticed that it was the tallest cypress speaking.

I'm going to escape, I thought and began to run in the direction of the avenue. But the cypress tore itself out of the earth by the roots, scattering dirt in all directions, and began to follow me. It's so much larger than me, I thought and stopped. The cypress stopped too. All its branches were shaking horribly—it was probably quite a while since it had last run.

"I accept," I said, and the cypress returned slowly to its hole.

I found the Queen lying in her great bed.

"I want to invite you to come for a stroll in the menagerie," I said, feeling pretty uncomfortable.

"But it's too early," she replied. "It isn't five o'clock yet. I never get up before ten."

"It's lovely out," I added.

"Oh, all right, if you insist."

We went down into the silent garden. Dawn is the time when nothing breathes, the hour of silence. Everything is transfixed, only the light moves. I sang a bit to cheer myself up. I was chilled to the bone. The Queen, in the meantime, was telling me that she fed all her horses on jam.

"It stops them from being vicious," she said.

She ought to have given the lions some jam, I thought to myself.

A long avenue, lined on both sides with fruit trees, led to the menagerie. From time to time a heavy fruit fell to the ground, Plop.

"Head colds are easily cured, if one just has the confidence," the Queen said. "I myself always take beef morsels marinated in olive oil. I put them in my nose. Next day the cold's gone. Or else, treated in the same way, cold noodles in liver juice, preferably calves' liver. It's a miracle how it dispels the heaviness in one's head."

She'll never have a head cold again, I thought.

"But bronchitis is more complicated. I nearly saved my poor husband from his last attack of bronchitis by knitting him a waistcoat. But it wasn't altogether successful."

We were drawing closer and closer to the menagerie. I could already hear the animals stirring in their morning slumbers. I would have liked to turn back, but I was afraid of the cypress and what it might be able to do with its hairy black branches. The more strongly I smelled the lion, the more loudly I sang, to give myself courage.

A Man in Love

Walking down a narrow street one evening, I stole a melon. The fruit seller, who was lurking behind his fruit, caught me by the arm.

"Miss, I've been waiting for a chance like this for forty years. For forty years I've hidden behind this pile of oranges in the hope that somebody might pinch some fruit. And the reason for that is this: I want to talk, I want to tell my story. If you don't listen, I'll hand you over to the police."

"I'm listening," I told him.

He took me by the arm and dragged me into the depths of his shop amongst the fruit and vegetables. We went through a door at the back and reached a room where there was a bed in which lay a woman, motionless and probably dead. It seemed to me that she must have been there a long time, for the bed was overgrown with grass.

"I water her every day," the greengrocer said

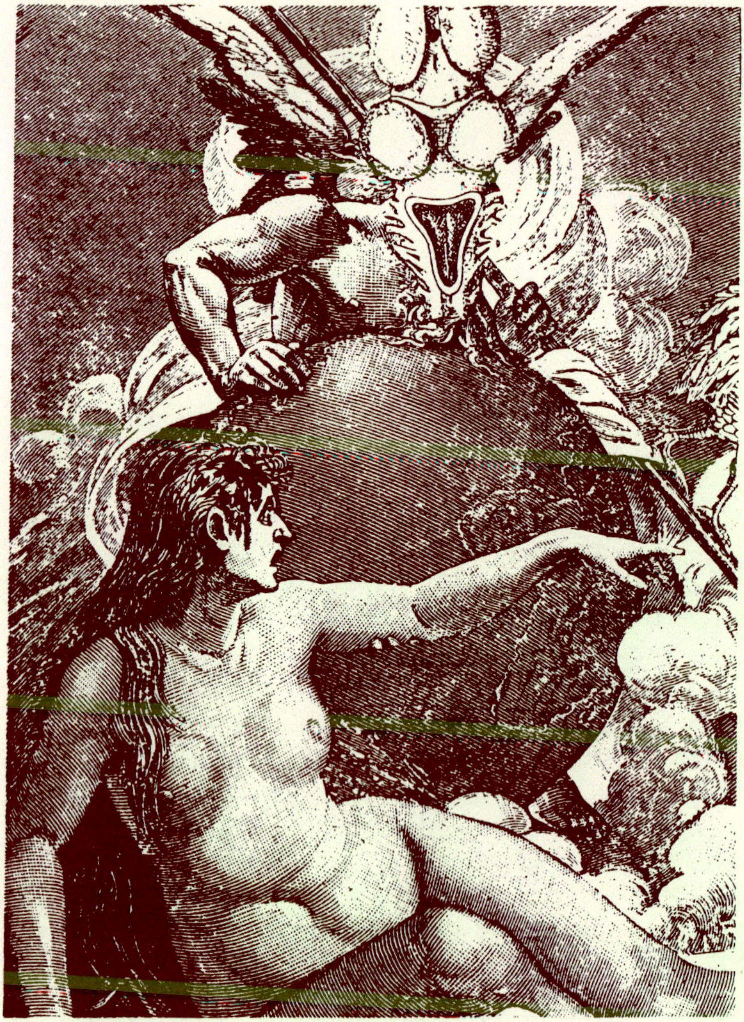

thoughtfully. "For forty years I've been quite unable to tell whether she is alive or dead. She hasn't moved or spoken or eaten during that time. But, and this is the strange thing, she remains warm. If you don't believe me, look."

Whereupon he lifted a corner of the bed cover and I saw a large number of eggs and some newly hatched chicks.

"You see," he said. "That's where I hatch my eggs. I sell fresh eggs too."

We sat down on opposite sides of the bed, and the greengrocer began to tell his tale.

"I love her so much, believe me, I've always loved her. She was so sweet. She had nimble little white feet. Would you like to see them?"

"No," I replied.

"Anyway," he continued with a deep sigh, "she was so beautiful! I had fair hair. But she, she had magnificent black hair. We both of us have white hair now. Her father was an extraordinary man. He had a big house in the country. He was a collector of lamb cutlets. The way we met was this. I have this special little gift. It's that I can dehydrate meat by just looking at it. Mr. Pushfoot (that was his name) heard about me. He asked me to come to his house to dehydrate his cutlets, so that they shouldn't rot. Agnes was his daughter. We immediately fell in love.

"We went away together in a boat on the Seine. I was rowing. Agnes said, 'I love you so much I live only for you.' And I used the same words to reply to her. I believe it's my love that keeps her so warm to this day. No doubt she is dead, but the warmth remains.

"Next year," he went on with a faraway look in his eyes, "next year I shall plant some tomatoes. I'd be surprised if they didn't do very well in there. . . .

"Night fell. I didn't know where we could pass our wedding night. Agnes had become so pale, so pale from exhaustion. At last, just as we left Paris behind, I saw a

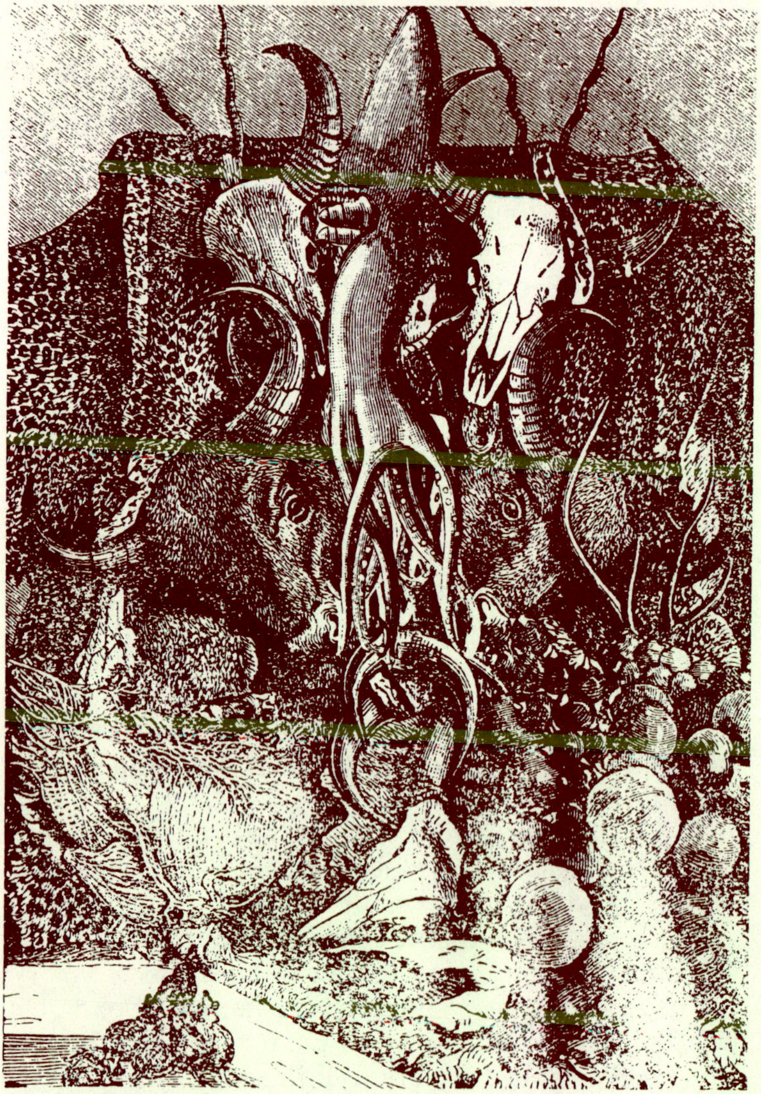

café beside the river. I moored the boat, and we walked up to the dark and sinister terrace. There were two wolves and a fox prowling around us. Nobody else. . . .

"I knocked. I knocked on the door, but it remained closed on a terrible silence.

" 'Agnes is tired! Agnes is very tired,' I shouted with all my might.

"Finally an old crone hung out of the window and said, 'I don't know a thing. It's the fox who's the landlord here. Let me sleep. You're getting on my nerves.'

"Agnes began to cry. There was nothing I could do but speak to the fox. 'Have you any beds?' I asked him several times. He didn't reply. He couldn't speak. Then the crone's head, now even older than before, came down slowly from the window, at the end of a piece of string.

" 'Speak to the wolves. I'm not in charge here. Please let me sleep.'

"I understood that the crone was mad, and that there was no sense in going on. Agnes was still weeping. I walked around the house several times and in the end managed to open a window through which we entered. We found ourselves in a high-ceilinged kitchen, where there was a large stove, glowing red with fire. Some vegetables were cooking themselves, jumping around in boiling water; this game delighted them. We ate well and afterwards lay down to sleep on the floor. I held Agnes in my arms. We didn't sleep a wink. There were all sorts of things in that terrible kitchen. A great number of rats sat on the threshold of their holes and sang with shrill, disagreeable little voices. Foul smells spread and dispersed one after the other, and there were strange draughts. I think it was the draughts that finished off my poor Agnes. She was never herself again. From that day on she spoke less and less. . . ."

At that, the owner of the fruit shop was so blinded by his tears that I was able to make my escape with my melon.

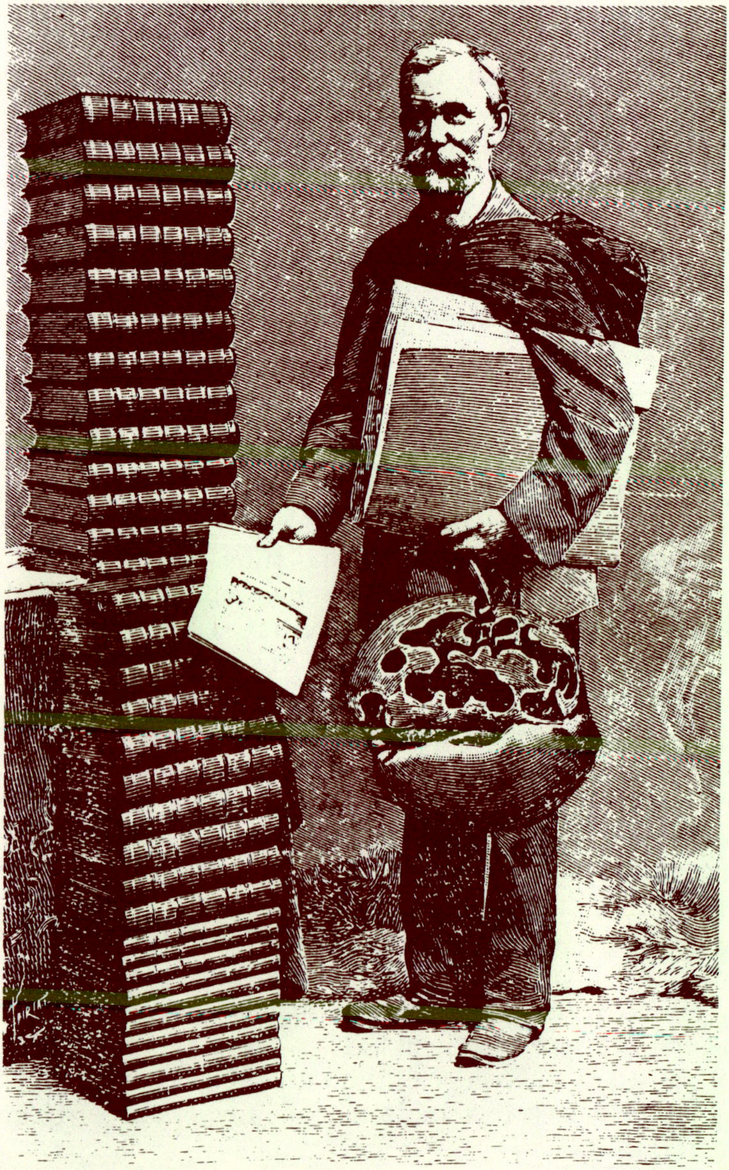

Uncle Sam Carrington

Whenever Uncle Sam Carrington saw the full moon he couldn't stop laughing. A sunset had the same effect on Aunt Edgeworth. Between them they caused my poor mother a great deal of suffering, for she had a certain social reputation to keep up.

When I was eight I was considered the most serious member of my family. My mother confided in me. She told me that it was a crying shame that she wasn't invited anywhere, that Lady Cholmondey-Bottom cut her when they passed in the street. I was grief stricken.

Uncle Sam Carrington and Aunt Edgeworth lived at home. They lived on the first floor. So it was impossible to hide our sad state of affairs. For days I wondered how I could deliver my family from this disgrace. In the end I couldn't stand the tension and my mother's tears, they upset me too much. I decided to find a solution by myself.

One evening, when the sun had turned a brilliant red, and Aunt Edgeworth was giggling in a particularly outrageous manner, I took a pot of jam and a fishing hook and set off. I sang, "Come into the garden, Maud, / For the black bat, night, has flown," to frighten the bats away. My father used to sing that when he didn't go to church, or else he sang a song called "It Cost Me Seven and Six Pence." He sang both with equal feeling.

All right, I thought to myself, the journey has begun. The night will surely bring a solution. If I keep count of the trees until I reach the place I'm going to, I shan't get lost. I'll remember the number of trees on the return journey.

But I'd forgotten that I could only count to ten, and even then I made mistakes. In a very short time I'd counted to ten several times, and I'd gone completely astray. Trees surrounded me on all sides. "I'm in a forest," I said, and I was right.

The full moon shone brightly between the trees, so I was able to see, a few yards in front of me, the origins of a distressing noise. It was two cabbages having a terrible fight. They were tearing each other's leaves off with such ferocity that soon there was nothing but torn leaves everywhere and no cabbages.

"Never mind," I told myself, "It's only a nightmare." But then I remembered suddenly that I'd never gone to bed that night, and so it couldn't possibly be a nightmare. "That's awful."

Thereupon I left the corpses and went on my way. Walking along I met a friend. It was the horse who, years later, was to play an important part in my life.

"Hello," he said. "Are you looking for something?" I explained to him the purpose of my late-night expedition.

"I can see that this is a very complicated matter from a social point of view," he said. "There are two ladies living near here who deal with such matters. Their aim is the extermination of family shame. They're expert at it. I'll take you to them if you like."

The Misses Cunningham-Jones lived in a house discretely surrounded by wild plants and underclothes of bygone times. They were in the garden, playing a game of draughts. The horse stuck his head between the legs of a pair of 1890 bloomers and addressed the Misses Cunningham-Jones.

"Show your friend in," said the lady sitting on the right, speaking with a very distinguished accent. "In the interest of respectability, we are always ready to come to the rescue." The other lady inclined her head graciously. She was wearing an immense hat decorated with a great collection of horticultural specimens.

"Young lady," she said, offering me a Louis Quinze chair, "does your family descend from our dear departed Duke of Wellington? Or from Sir Walter Scott, that noble aristocrat of pure literature?"

I felt a bit embarrassed. There were no aristocrats in my family. She saw my hesitation and said with the most charming smile, "My dear child, you must realise that here we deal only with the affairs of the oldest and most noble families of England."

I had an inspiration, and my face lit up. "In our dining room at home . . ."

The horse kicked me hard in the backside. "Never mention anything as vulgar as food," he whispered.

Fortunately the ladies were slightly deaf. I immediately corrected myself. "In our drawing room," I continued, confused, "there is a table on which, we are told, a duchess forgot her lorgnette in 1700."

"In that case," one of the ladies said, "we can perhaps settle the matter. Of course, we shall have to set a rather higher fee."

"Wait here for a few minutes, then we'll give you what you need. While you are waiting, you may look at the pictures in this book. It is instructive and interest-

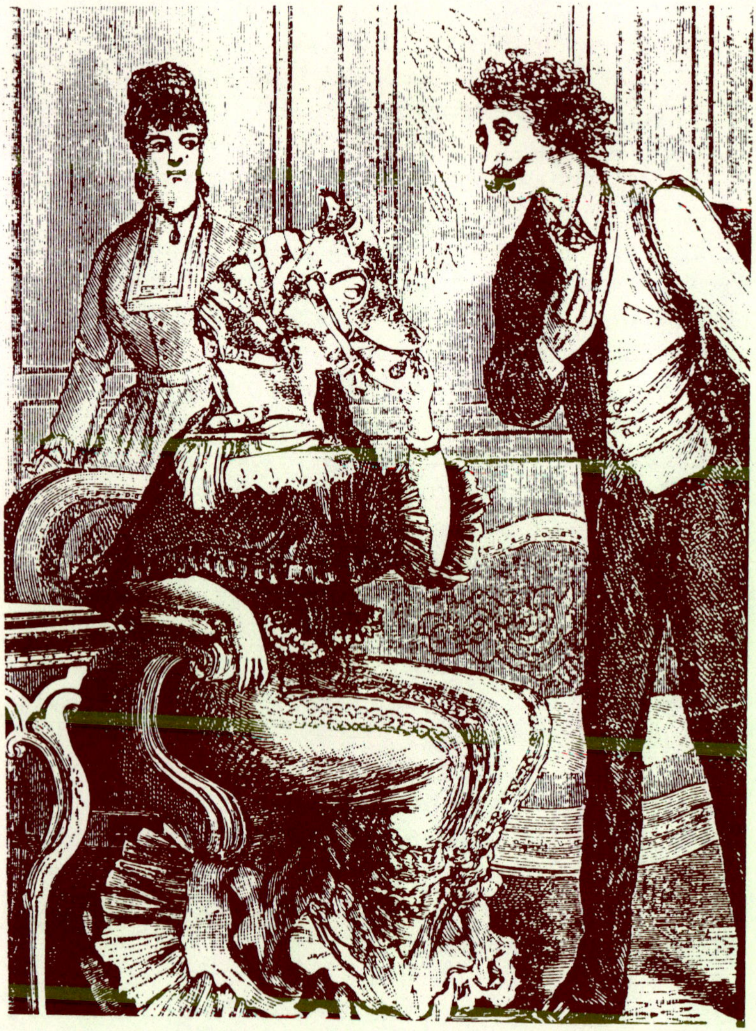

ing. No library is complete without it: my sister and I have always lived by its admirable example."

The book was called *The Secrets of the Flowers of Refinement, or The Vulgarity of Food.*

When the two ladies had gone, the horse said, "Do you know how to walk without making a sound?"

"Certainly," I replied.

"Let's go and see the ladies at work," he said. "Come. But if you value your life, don't make the slightest noise."

The ladies were in their kitchen garden. It was behind their house and was surrounded by a high brick wall. I climbed on the horse's back, and a pretty astonishing sight met my eyes: the Misses Cunningham-Jones, each armed with a huge whip, were whipping the vegetables on all sides, shouting, "One's got to suffer to go to Heaven. Those who do not wear corsets will never get there."

The vegetables, for their part, were fighting among themselves, and the larger ones threw the smaller ones at the ladies with cries of hate.

"It's always like this," said the horse in a low voice. "The vegetables have to suffer for the sake of society. You'll see that they'll soon catch one for you, and that it'll die for the cause."

The vegetables didn't look keen to die an honourable death, but the ladies were stronger. Soon two carrots and a courgette fell into their hands.

"Quick," said the horse, "let's go back."

We had hardly got back and were sitting once more in front of *The Vulgarity of Food* when the two ladies returned, looking just about as poised as before. They gave me a parcel which contained the vegetables, and in return I paid them with the pot of jam and the fishing hook.

LITTLE FRANCIS

Little Francis

"Musical instruments are bodies out of space," said the father. They were under the dome in the Salle Liszt. The orchestra had got half through the fifth *Brandenburg* Concerto.

"Like God?" said Amelia.

"No, not like God, they're far more beautiful and were there before God was invented. They're like cones and spheres and triangles and rectangles. They were always there, they weren't invented, they were discovered. They're like stars and planets."

"Reverend Mother says, 'Honor thy father and thy mother.' How can I obey her when you tell such wicked lies?"

"You are becoming a little prude."

"Father, I shall scream."

"Scream then."

Silence.

"You know I'm not to be thwarted, that's what the doctor says. I dreamed I saw Mummy in Heaven last night. Is Mummy in Heaven?"

"I shouldn't think so."

"Is she in Hell?"

"Neither. She is probably a multiplication table in space or a new sort of violin not yet discovered, or a circle around a planet."

"Sometimes I think you are a devil, Father."

"Really? Well I'm very glad you don't take me for an angel."

"Why don't you want to be an angel?"

"Because I should be bored. I would rather be a pointed cone whizzing diabolically in space and singing like a flute."

"Why do people go to concerts?"

"To practice difficult ways of supporting their heads on their hands."

"I came to wear my new chiffon."

"Yes, they do that too. It's very much like going to church and almost as depressing."

"I thought you liked music."

"I do. I think Bach and Mozart should be listened to under cheerful circumstances, not in an atmosphere of boredom."

"What are they going to play next?"

"The sixth *Brandenburg* Concerto."

"Here they come. The music is going to begin."

Halfway through the little girl uttered a piercing scream. "Father, Father, something dreadful is going to happen to me!" All faces turned in their direction.

"I saw a magpie fly out of one of the violins."

"It's not big enough to hold a magpie. Are you sure it wasn't the piano it came from?"

"I'm going to faint; I know something awful is going to happen."

"Here they come to ask us to go out. Amelia, you are a dreadful nuisance."

On the way home they met an accident. A dead horse was lying in the road. Amelia screamed: "Look, look, look at the horrible blood pouring and pouring out of the big hole in his head!" And she jumped out of the taxi.

"I followed her," said Hector. "We went to Fontainebleau but she slipped me and took the next train back. All the time we had awful scenes. She kept shouting for Daddy. Then last night after the house was locked up she went out looking for a bishop till about two in the morning and then lay on the steps of Notre Dame till she was found by a policeman and apparently told him she was waiting for the Angel of Death. She seems to think you a swine for not letting her be confirmed. This morning she demolished three bicycles in the workroom, with a hatchet. She said it was to avenge herself on you for not coming home. She's busy confessing now, feeling some remorse over the bicycles."

"That's awful," said Uncle Ubriaco. "Amelia has bouts like this. She's so nervous."

Francis felt depressed. "Perhaps I'd better go to a hotel?" he suggested.

"No, you stay," said Uncle Ubriaco.

Amelia arrived, a little girl with plaits. "You're here at last, Daddy," she said. They kissed each other. "And who is this?"

"That's your cousin Francis."

She looked at Francis coldly.

"And are we then never to have that holiday on our own?"

Uncle Ubriaco looked embarrassed.

"Take me out for a walk, Father. I have something to say to you in private."

"Well, it won't be long. Excuse me, Francis. Wouldn't you like to take a bath? I shall be back in twenty minutes."

Francis had a cold bath and amused himself around the house, coming at last to the workroom. This was a spacious apartment on the ground floor filled with half-constructed constructions and wholly demolished bicycles. The walls were lined with bookshelves that held books, spare tyres, bottles of oil, chipped figureheads, spanners, hammers, and reels of thread. He began to read the titles of the first row of books, which were dusty but in good order: *Man and Bicycle*, *Intricacies of Pedals*, *Hans Andersen's Fairy Tales*, *Tobson's Essays on Spokes and Bells*, *Free Wheels and Ball Bearings*, *The Oxford Dictionary*, etc.

Then Francis had the idea that he would like to cool his feet on the stone floor, so he took off his shoes and stockings and wandered around looking at Uncle Ubriaco's interesting collection of things. There was for instance a pair of starved cockroaches in a small cage, a string of artificial onions astoundingly true to life (they must have been made of china), a spinning wheel that worked, ladies' corsets of complicated pattern, and a great many cogwheels. Francis was rather tempted to try on a particular corset, a black one with faded purple lace and roses worked in gold thread. It was the matter of a moment to slip the corset over his head: it reached below his knees but by lacing tightly it made quite a nice fit around the waist.

He closed his eyes and tried to imagine a pair of ample, warm thighs in place of his own rather thin legs, only to be seen from the knee downwards. He was interrupted by Amelia opening the door. "What are you doing in here?" she said angrily, advancing. "Only Father and I are allowed in the workroom."

"Don't shout," said Francis.

"Listen! Father and I are going away tomorrow. You're to go straight back to England."

"Yes," said Francis, picking his way with difficulty towards his shoes. "When your father tells me to go."

"You are to go now," she screamed. "I cannot tolerate looking at your horrible long toenails!"

Francis controlled his temper by glancing at his feet. His toenails were rather long. "Listen," he said, "I don't mind going to a hotel. You live here. Anyhow, I never could stand being shouted at." He tried bending over to pick up his shoes but the corset was laced too tightly.

"And take off Father's corset!" Amelia's voice rose another semitone.

"Father's corset?" said Francis with a smile.

"Father is very childish," yelled the little girl. "And you are a dirty little idiot. I won't have him mixing with people like you."

"Perhaps he likes it," suggested Francis, unlacing himself. "You probably bore him."

"Nasty brat! You're heartless! Why don't you leave Father and me to our own peaceful life? We don't want people like you messing around. You don't seem to realise I'm very very ill." She paused dramatically. "Very ill—I'm dying—I've got only a few months to live—leave Father and me together for our last few months. I shall be dead soon."

"I am sure you bore him," said Francis. "Dead people are bad enough, but half dead people who scream into the bargain—!" No doubt Amelia would have thrown *The Oxford Dictionary* at Francis at that moment had not Uncle Ubriaco entered. "Go to bed, Amelia," he said, taking in the scene at a glance. "I won't have you shouting at Francis."

"I won't go to bed. No! Never never never while that filthy swine is here."

Francis gave Uncle Ubriaco a weary smile and said, "I'm off to a hotel."

"All right," said Uncle Ubriaco, trying to make himself heard above Amelia's kicking and screaming: she seemed to be having some kind of a fit on the floor. He bent down and whispered rapidly into Francis's ear: "Café de Flore, Boulevard Saint-Germain, in an hour's time."

Eventually Francis reached the appointed place and sat down at a table. He remembered he had no French money but knew that in France you could have a drink and pay an hour later, so he thought it safe to order a cocoa. "No cocoa," said the waiter contemptuously. "*Café au lait, thé, tisane. Pas de* cocoa. *Chocolat* if you like."

"Well, wine," said Francis nervously.

"*Blanc ou rouge,*" snapped the waiter.

Francis supposed he was being insulted so he said, "*Je aussi.*"

"*Blanc ou rouge,*" grated the waiter, "red or white?"

Francis blushed. "Red, with a biscuit," and he turned away, pretending to contemplate the boulevard in an offhand fashion.

"English boy?" said a young woman, sitting down opposite Francis so suddenly that he jumped. "I went to England. What a lovely place! I stayed near Southampton. It was oh so green!"

"Yes, I suppose it's green," said Francis regaining his composure. "But they say it is much greener in Ireland."

"Oh yes? But no! Nothing could be so green, so very very green as those fields, as if they have lights under the ground. I am Charlotte. What is your name? And do buy me a drink."

"I am Francis. What would you like? I wonder if you wouldn't mind ordering yourself? You see my French is no good."

"My aunt was English you know; she had many big

books in which she would press insects. Mosquitoes, ants, and caterpillars, all she found in those lovely green fields! What a pity I have to earn my living the way I do! English people are funny about these things, you know. But I can see you are *gentil!*"

"It depends which way you see things," replied Francis. "I expect you do quite well, though?"

"I have ups and downs. The season is rather poor this year, though we are all expecting prices to go up with the Exhibition coming on."

"Yes, that ought to be a good thing," said Francis thoughtfully. "They say a lot of foreigners will be in Paris."

"I must brush up my Australian," said Charlotte. "They say languages make all the difference. Do you know if Australian is difficult?"

"I think it's almost exactly like English. Unless of course you want to learn Maori?"

"No. Just a smattering of Australian. I shan't mind the grammar. One or two irregular verbs of course and a good vocabulary. That's all I shall need. You see I have ambitions, in my own way."

"I quite understand," said Francis. "But I really think you would do better to learn perhaps a little Russian? There are bound to be a lot of Russians; they have a pavilion, you know."

"I think Australian is more distinguished," said Charlotte. "The Russians over here are mostly without money."

They talked on pleasantly for an hour or more till Uncle Ubriaco came. His eyes looked tired, and he had a long perpendicular scratch from his right eye to the corner of his mouth. Charlotte said *"Bonsoir"* and hurried off. Uncle Ubriaco sat down and sighed.

"I think we'd better leave tomorrow morning," he said at last. "And maybe you had better go to a hotel tonight." Francis agreed.

"I know a small place where you will be comfortable. I will call for you at six-thirty. An early start might be prudent."

"I think it might," said Francis.

On the road south, taken in easy stages, Francis improved his French. At alternate kilometres Uncle Ubriaco made him sing the verbs *to be* and *to have* to the respective tunes of "Rule, Britannia" and "Onward, Christian Soldiers." In the evenings they had conversation and vocabulary exercises, during which Uncle Ubriaco read Francis the poems of Hans Arp and the novels of Rabelais.

The weather became slowly warmer, and one evening in a mounting thunderstorm they came upon the South: announced by an agitated chorus of crickets trilling and chirping. The air was alive with noise, yet it did not disturb the heavy silence of the approaching night.

This is me, I must be careful, thought Francis. The next day they went over the hills and down into a plain and rode all through the day, coming upon a river with a white stony shore. Francis had never seen such water, so brilliant and deep and green. In the evening they crossed a long, narrow bridge and turned sharp right into the village of Saint-Roc. It was just light enough to see two hedgehogs squashed in the middle of the road.

There were three cafés in the village: Café du Pont, Hôtel du Centre, and Café Pirigou. The first two were full up owing to the coming fête, so they were obliged to try the Café Pirigou. It had a terrace looking out onto the dusty square. The woman inside wore a short skirt and thick woollen leggings ending in a pair of carpet slippers. She wasn't clean.

"I have two beds," she said. "No lavatory, no bathroom, and no food." She talked as though Francis and Ubriaco were hard of hearing.

"Why no food?" asked Uncle Ubriaco. "Don't you eat?"

"I eat all right," she said with a loud laugh. "But you don't."

Uncle Ubriaco waited patiently for her mirth to cease. "Why not?"

"My mother," she explained, wiping her eyes, "is old and ill and suffers horribly. Often she screams all night long. So she can't cook and I don't want any more work than I can help. But you can eat *chez la Marie.*" The woman jerked her thumb over her right shoulder. "Next door. It's also the *bureau de tabac.* La Marie herself calls it Hôtel du Centre."

"You had better show us your room." But she had caught sight of Ubriaco's bicycles, Roger of Kildare and Darling Little Mabel, and ignored his request.

"How magnificent," she exclaimed. "You'll let me have a ride someday?"

"Certainly," said Uncle Ubriaco. "I would be charmed."

"I have a lover in Avignon who dropped me three months ago. I'd certainly like to visit him. He works in a bank."

"We will do that," said Uncle Ubriaco. "And now the room."

"The room is very dirty at the moment, but I can clean it. After my last five clients the sheets—!"

"You might change them," said Francis usefully. "You might even wash them."

The room was pleasant, if dirty, and inhabited by several scorpions and a host of flies. One corner was given over to strings of dry garlic, a sack of potatoes, and a disused stove.

"It's all right," said Ubriaco, "till we find a tent. We intend to camp on the other side of the river."

The terrace at la Marie's was covered with vines, and she had a large mole on her chin, decorated with three grey hairs. Her manner was ingratiating: she mauled

Francis's buttocks. "I can give you some hors d'oeuvres, rabbit cooked in thyme and its own guts, goat's cheese and fruit."

They sat where they could see the river and the tall calcareous cliffs opposite. The rocks were shaped after a hundred different creatures.

"I used to know a man who passed his whole life making the landscape into a zoo," said Uncle Ubriaco dreamily. "He worked for years making rocks into lions and tigers, cabinet ministers, centaurs, historical characters, etc. He was a charming fellow but worked too hard. I think cypress trees are delightful, they remind me of wigs, and as they usually grow in cemeteries one imagines some beautiful lady's death's-head underneath."

Two people sat down at the next table. They talked with a strong Marseillais accent. Ubriaco joined their conversation. "So you are camping?"

"Yes, by the side of the river. The peasants say it's dangerous to camp on the stones as the river can rise in the night if it rains in the mountains. However"—with a deprecatory laugh—"the weather seems sure enough and we're returning to Marseilles in two days."

"And your tent?" Uncle Ubriaco became interested. "Don't you want to sell it?" They exchanged a muttered dialogue, and the affair was transacted. In three days Uncle Ubriaco was to become the possessor of a medium-sized khaki tent.

Rosaline Pirigou was shouting in the kitchen when they got in. Her old mother was crouching by the fire, her flat yellow face twisted with rage.

"Why, in the name of God, don't you get to bed instead of pitying yourself beside the fire all day?"

"*Salope!*" screamed the crone. "My poor stomach is putrifying with pain and you make my life a misery."

"So much the better," returned Rosaline, loud but without ill feeling. "Why don't you hang yourself then?

Better people than you have hanged themselves before now. There's a tree outside and rope is cheap."

"You send a poor suffering old woman to her death! While I bore you in my belly, I ought to have drowned myself! Before it was too late."

"Well you didn't," said Rosaline. "So it's about time you stop nagging and get to bed. Come. I'll take off your belt." The old lady lifted a black-, purple-, and green-knitted petticoat before she arrived at a pair of long elastic-legged knickers. It was like the peeling of some curious artichoke. Rosaline delivered her of a heavily upholstered stomach belt. The old one passed two withered hands over her round stomach and rolled her eyes at Uncle Ubriaco. "If you only knew how I suffer!" She grabbed Francis by the arm and shoved her face forward. "You are young. Stay young and happy! Whereas I! Ah God, all night and all day I groan with pain!"

"Get to bed Mother," shouted Rosaline from the sink. "Stop talking. Go up and I'll prepare your *cataplasme*."

Muttering, the old lady fingered Francis's arm like a searching insect, then took the small oil lamp from the table and made her way upstairs painfully.

The other side of the river was a different world from the village side. In the shadow of the overhanging monsters, Uncle Ubriaco pitched his tent with an unprofessional hand. He cleared away some of the stones and made a bed of sand. The tent stood up like an impertinent pocket handkerchief. A few yards off, the river rushed white over the stones, broke into a deep green pool, and sailed on smooth and wide. The pool was the deepest point on the river for a hundred yards. A rock like a big mushroom stood in the middle, sinking into the stones beneath.

Francis sat on the edge of the pool where it was shallow, washing his teeth. Little fishes breakfasted on the toothpaste and saliva that he spat into the water. He was thinking about the warmth and the water around him and the other village, not Saint-Roc, that grew from a high cliff, upriver. It was white with towers and black with cypress trees but seemed deserted.

"I think one should go there," he said to Ubriaco, who was pretending to be a sea snake on the mushroom.

"It's very hot today," he replied, raising himself elegantly on his hind legs or tail and waving his arms absently. "And in an hour's time it will be hotter still." He disappeared into the water with a plop. His head appeared a moment later, smooth and wet. "And I don't like walking on hot days. I don't mind swimming or flying or sleeping or even drinking. But I don't like walking." His voice grew fainter as he swam off.

"We could swim there," said Francis, as the white head came into earshot.

"We can't swim up the cliff," replied Uncle Ubriaco reasonably.

"No we can't swim up the cliff," said Francis pensively. He watched Ubriaco play shadowing games under the water with a cloud of little fishes around his head.

Near midday Uncle Ubriaco emerged from the pool. His eyes were still like two beautiful blue fish; his hair dried into fluffy white plumes in the sun. He stretched himself out on the stones near Francis. "What in the world do I love more than warm stones," he murmured, caressing his belly. "And water? What a sweet life we are living, Francis. I would like to catch some of those little fish and fry them. They're very good to eat." He continued with a cruel smile, "You sprinkle them with lemon and they crackle between your teeth. I feel hungry now. Go and get that cheese from the tent. There are some tomatoes too and some bread in the tin box; the wine is in the pool near the tent." He closed his eyes.

Francis came back, and they ate lazily amongst an

appreciative hoard of flies. After lunch they both slept. When Francis awoke, stupefied by the sun, he saw the village upstream, going purple with shadow. Uncle Ubriaco was snoring a series of peculiar wistful notes that only he could produce: Francis felt he could dance to the rhythm. Soon Uncle Ubriaco awoke as well, with an unconscious smile. "We can go to your village. I don't mind going there now," he said.

A small path led up to a ruined arch. The nearer they got to Mâze, the village, the more lonely it became. Ancient scrap iron of unknown origin lay in the dust. Beyond the arch, the little streets were as dark as night. Here and there wild fig trees pushed up inside the cottages. A stray billy goat walked out from a front door and stood proudly in his stink and cortege of flies, looking at them with reptilian eyes. Slowly he strolled around the strangers and disappeared into another house: he was the only living being they saw.

A flight of steps led up to a door of Gothic shape. Only the door could be seen, for the building itself was hidden between two cottages. They mounted the steps and came into a chapel, one wall of which was unhewn rock. The three other walls were new but unfinished, and the windows had no glass.

"The rock wall is for apparitions," said Uncle Ubriaco. "Someday we will come and live here." Through an opening was a small garden and a wall that separated it from the void where, fathoms below, ran the river.

They went out and looked at the world below.

"This is a wonderful place to live," agreed Francis, sighing. "We could both dress up as bishops and solemnise Black Masses in the rock." He closed his eyes ecstatically and saw himself and Ubriaco dressed in purple, wearing huge mitres and carrying ornate sceptres to coax devils out of the rock. He saw the villagers of Saint-Roc staring, whispering in fear as from a distance a tall figure dressed in purple (himself) was wafted out of deserted Mâze and hung suspended in midair uttering incantations. A few minutes later another figure, taller still, with a chalice and accompanied by ten or more black shapes, would sail with dignity thrice in circles and, turning upside down, murmur soft abuse on humanity below. He saw the parish priest preaching in whispers to his pale-faced congregation in the church in Saint-Roc, now and again pointing a trembling finger over his left shoulder.

When he turned away from this delicious reverie, Francis saw Uncle Ubriaco wandering around, humming and picking what Francis took to be flowers. Actually they were little prickly herbs with an extremely sweet odor. "There is a legend in this district," said Ubriaco, binding a large bunch of the herbs, "that once there was an extremely ugly girl, so hideous nobody could look her straight in the face. So she was obliged to go about in a veil. However, she had very lovely hair and one dark night a wizard is said to have fallen in love with the smell of her hair; in the morning he was so horrified by her face that he buried her—all except the hair. These herbs are the result. They're called *miraldalocks.*"

Francis took a deep breath from the herbs, and his head reeled slightly. "What a heavy smell."

"When I'm plucking miraldalocks, I always imagine I'm everlastingly safe from not being drunk." Uncle Ubriaco seemed to be talking to himself. "I think we have nearly enough now. Let me see, we'll need a flat stone and a round stone. The sun's going down. We must hurry before it gets too dark."

Francis followed him through the obscure village, sniffing now and then at his fingers that had pressed the sweet miraldalocks. Down below was the tent; Ubriaco found the stones shaped as he wanted and bid Francis light a wax candle. Cross-legged at the door of the tent, he pounded the herbs between the two stones.

"You see," he explained to Francis's shape that sat

silently, a little way off, his back to the river, "they really make such nice cigarettes. So much cheaper and better. All we need is some rice paper, which is easily found in the village."

When he had pounded enough, he took a little stone jar and with a knife scraped the sticky remains of the squashed miraldalocks into it. Then he made a little fire around the jar. The mixture smelt delightful.

"Icker lackle bluebottle," he quoted.

Icker lacker lout.
The light in the jar
Is the true light and way
For the feet of the beet
Which with endless entreat
Wring the heart and the teat
Of the onions from Tartar.

"That's one of my own poems," he explained, getting to his feet. "I composed it a year ago, while listening to the *Eine kleine Nachtmusik* in the Albert Hall. I was thinking of my motherland—you see I get so homesick at times . . .

"We really must have dinner soon. Come, we'll cross the river before my stomach falls out on the floor. That fire will go on till we return, and it ought to be ready by then." They paddled across the river, which in the middle only reached to their knees.

Rosaline was standing on her terrace when they arrived in the square.

"You haven't been to see me for three days," she yelled. "If you like I'll cook you a dinner."

On the steps of the terrace sat a little boy in a paper hat; he smoked a cheroot and spat now and again towards his sister's profile; she could not see, for her eye was blind on that side of her face. She was sitting in a chair with her hands lying idly in her lap. Rosaline ignored the pair of them. "You must not forget me," she said, grinning at Francis. "Go buy some food. I can make you an omelette, or some aubergines in tomato sauce."

"Aubergines would be nice," replied Ubriaco. "Where do we buy them?"

"In the garden of the lady opposite," said Rosaline. "She'll pick them off the plant so you can get them fresh."

The lady emerged enormous from her house, with a spiky pair of scissors in hand. She waddled around her aubergine plants and selected two fat purple globes that hung amongst their prickly leaves.

"Those are nice chaps," she admitted, "but we want some rain." She presented Francis with the two. "The tomatoes," she continued, poking around in the dark. "How many?"

"Six."

"Here then, and I have some nice lettuce."

"Give us some as well."

They returned to Rosaline Pirigou like queens of the May. She disappeared into the kitchen.

Francis and Uncle Ubriaco sat on the terrace with their two silent companions. Ubriaco offered the half-blind girl a cigarette, which she refused and accepted at the same time. She was called Claire, she said. What did she do? Ah, she amused herself and looked after her father's goats. Her father was the village undertaker—that was him coming now, the dark man. He arrived and sat down and also took a cigarette. Soon the younger sister arrived, a girl of fifteen carrying an infant. There were two more small staring infants, members of the same family, all very quiet. Soon Rosaline came out and set down a dish of aubergines, cooked to a turn, like fish in red sauce.

"Here we have the undertaker," she remarked, staring at the whole family aggressively. "If you want to be measured for a coffin here and now, Francis, he's your man." The undertaker got up and walked into the café.

"You see little Élise here," continued Rosaline, undaunted, pointing out the sister of fifteen, "she's a mother already, poor little thing."

"That's right," said Élise, patting her infant.

"And her little sister of eight got raped by the same man. Wasn't he the father of your second child too, Claire?"

"That's right," said Claire, puffing her cigarette.

"He's a dirty chap," said Rosaline, sitting down next to Uncle Ubriaco. "Always drunk around the village. I hardly like selling him drinks myself, but one must live. He had a go at me, but I kicked him in the parts he needed most! Pierre de Trignan, they call him. At the time Élise had her baby, there was a big stir because an old gentleman of eighty hanged himself. The story got around that he was frightened of de Trignan." The two girls nodded together. "We had gendarmes in the village and all sorts. He hanged himself from this very tree," she added, pointing up into the branches. "How such an old chap ever got up there we never could tell, but there he was when I opened my shutters in the morning, swinging about in front of my very nose, and black in the face! My goodness he was dead! I gave a scream and woke my mother who screamed too and there we were screaming, name of a dog! with poor old Édouard dangling like a bunch of bad grapes outside!" The whole family nodded sadly.

"That's the way it was," said Claire, blinking her good eye. "And we thought we'd never see the end of those *sacré* gendarmes. Morning, noon, and night in everybody's business." And she relapsed into her habitual silence.

One by one the family disappeared, a dissolving circle of faces, until Francis and Uncle Ubriaco were alone with Rosaline.

"They're a bad family," said Rosaline, picking her teeth. "Terrible robbers all of them."

"Perhaps they're poor?" suggested Ubriaco, who felt

attracted to the undertaker's children and their children. "Anyhow, I don't believe in work."

"They'd take that nice watch of yours like that!" said Rosaline, snapping her fingers. "Many's the pair of knickers, spoons, and glasses that have gone the same way!" She turned to an old man who was sitting quietly in the corner.

"Isn't that so, Simon?"

"Ahhh," murmured the old man, staring in front of him with docile eyes and rolling cigarettes with his absently moving fingers.

"Simon had a nice pair of Sunday trousers swiped. Eh Simon?"

"Ahhh." He cast a sweet, vague look over Francis and Uncle Ubriaco and then seemed to forget them.

"Simon is too old to talk," explained Rosaline. "But he listens to everything everybody says and drinks too much. Go and get me a bucket of water, Simon."

"Mummmmmmm." The old man toddled off to the pump and came back tottering with the weight of the bucket. Then he sat down and took up his reverie where he had left off.

"Silly with age," remarked Rosaline. "But a nice old chap all the same."

The village clock struck. Francis and Ubriaco got up to go.

"Well, have a good night," said Rosaline, "and don't get drowned on the way over." She laughed aloud and patted Uncle Ubriaco's arm. "Tomorrow Simon will bring you some figs from 'the Club Simon.' He has some nice fat rabbits up there too. Eh Simon?"

"Ahhhh mmmm."

"And I'll cook you a rabbit one night. I know just how to do it."

They returned to the tent by moonlight after Ubriaco had bought several little books of rice paper for rolling cigarettes. The water flowed quietly past them. The embers were still glowing around the little stone pot, and the atmosphere was sweet with smell for yards around. Crickets vibrated excitedly as they examined the mixture: it had hardened into half-sticky, half-crackly lumps. Uncle Ubriaco cooled the little jar in the river—a cloud of steam rose up where he soused it. Then he came back and rolled the cooked miraldalocks into neat cigarettes.

"You'll see first how nice these are," he said, lighting them each a cigarette. "Tomorrow I really ought to get a letter from Hector; I would like to know how things are in Paris. I wonder if Hector ever learned to write?"

"I can't say," said Francis distantly, for his own voice seemed to come from a part of himself at least twenty feet above his head. "I don't really think it matters though."

"Ah but it does," replied Uncle Ubriaco, far away in the cliffs. "For how can I get any news if Hector can't write?"

"Telephone," squeaked the voice almost inaudibly, so far had it flown.

"But telephoning is so expensive," said Ubriaco, hollowly, and they were standing together outside the chapel in the little garden. "Besides I don't want her to know my telephone number."

Francis went down to look at a clump of miraldalocks.

"I think I ought to pull that up. You haven't got a telephone number."

He grasped the herbs and started to force them slowly out of the ground.

"I know, but the village is so small she'd find us at once. That wouldn't do at all." The herbs were followed by a woman's head and shoulders. The earth broke away as Francis tugged with no great effort. "Well, I've got Miraldalocks," he said, turning. "But she doesn't look too alive."

"No," replied Uncle Ubriaco pensively. "That means

you've not taken quite enough. Of course, Hector knows the address, but I don't think he's ass enough to give us away."

"I hope not," said Francis, supporting Miraldalocks with one hand. But Miraldalocks was heavy and started slipping inertly back into the earth.

"Do you think she'd come looking for us here?" said Francis, as all of Miraldalocks gradually disappeared—except of course for her hair. "I think it might be very unpleasant if she did come."

His voice had developed the curious habit of winging softly around him in ever-decreasing circles. He could see Ubriaco's voice doing the same thing. Ubriaco's was a palish blue, with one red eye, while his own was black and green. They joined each other above their respective owners' heads and played a graceful game of mignonette.

"It must be avoided." They had perched on a tree nearly out of earshot, but the words were distinguishable.

"However, one's all right here. Really more than all right. Rosaline's cuisine is really very good in a simple way."

"I've never been so happy," said his own voice, so trembling with emotion that it would have fallen off the branch had it not had the presence of mind to grab a leaf. "So much the better," replied Uncle Ubriaco's.

The letter from Hector arrived accordingly, the following morning. The handwriting seemed to be the work of a person suffering from brain damage. It read:

Dear Sir
 Having to render thanks for your communication of the 13 inst. and moreover to state koncerning the individual in question such news as it pleezes you to arsk.

(a) scenes of an active nature imediately ensueing your departure. (i.e. tears, threats on your own person and the person of your neview. Screaming and praying.) The damadges ammount to aproximately 2 bicykles, one window, an Adam table, and a reseptikle for drink (placed on already mentioned table) The cat, (expiring shortly after grievious head wounds administered with the foot) and numbrous omaments dating from Her Majesty Victoria (R.I.P.)

(b) Lucid period lasting 24 hrs. within which time the person in question visits the war minister (without success) enquiring your whereabouts. Also the general post office and the police station. Supplying on each call an ample collection of photographs and personal apparel. etc.

(c) of late has become silent with intervals of weeping and lamentations on your kidney trouble which, she is convinced will end in death, what with your asosiating with people of a vulger character. etc.

(d) and lastly sir a letter to the pope ordering 50 litres of holy water to be sent from Rome and delivered hear at the erliest opportunity.

I must add that there is a pressing request that there might be a letter addressed to the person herself hereby in your own handriting reasuring her of your good health and progress of erlier mentioned kidney trouble.

Your alarm klok is mended and what is left of the geraniums in the Hall are doing nicely.

I, am, believe me Deer sir, Yours very truely
Hector.

They were sitting on Rosaline's terrace taking a morning aperitif. It was the day of the fête, and the square was filled with caravans, dogs, roundabouts, and paper decorations—a sweating mixture in the heat. Claire walked by driving a pair of goats. She stopped in front of them and smiled, her blind eye whitish and serious, then she mooned on. Rosaline had her hair in papers and wore two perfect geometrical circles of rouge on each cheek. She was leaning on the balustrade, presenting a large flattish bottom to Ubriaco and Francis.

"There'll be some doings tonight in the bushes," she reflected over her left shoulder. "Claire takes five francs a time."

"Don't you ever make love?" asked Ubriaco, unseating a fly from his nose.

Rosaline let out a mouthful of air between her lips with a realistic sound.

"Me? Not now! All my life I've only loved my banker—otherwise, phut!"

"And your husband?"

"I only lived with him a month, drunken pig. Tonight there'll be dancing in the square. We'll have a java together, eh?"

"Yes," said Uncle Ubriaco. "I dance the java extremely well. Francis will serve in the café while we're dancing."

Towards evening they traversed the river once more, into the turmoil of spitting, sweating, bobbing humanity. The orchestra made deliberate music, each musician going his own way, regardless of his fellows. The dust was so churned up that from the knee downwards the dancers were invisible. Still they worked away, extracting as much sweat as possible from their respective partners. The smell was terrific.

Café Pirigou was packed with totally inebriated peasants. Rosaline presided regally, decked out in all the reds, blues, yellows, and greens under the sun. Her hairdo was fantastic. She had great dark patches of sweat under each arm, where the colors ran into weird confusion.

"I thought you were slipping out of that java," she

yelled happily down a tray of *bocs* and *diavolos*. "*Sainte Vierge!* You'd have caught it if you didn't come!

"Hey, you, Old Jean, take this tray! And tell Simon to hurry on with the clean glasses. I'm going to dance with this gentleman." She gripped Uncle Ubriaco in a living vice and maneuvered him out of sight. Francis found himself drinking with a group of vicious-looking individuals and joining in a chorus of the *chanson nationale.* Joseph took the solos with enormous volume, his face worn into a semishapeless lump from all the tomatoes thrown at it: this was his sole occupation. Francis was called upon for an English song, so he gave them "Hark! Hark! the Lark" in a doubtful treble, "Who Is Silvia?" and "Pussy Cat, Pussy Cat, Where Have You Been?"

He had just reached the last line of the first stanza when an extraordinary face bobbed into view over the balcony. Obviously a woman, thought Francis, stopping abruptly at "I caught a little mouse—" She was staring straight into his face, and he felt he knew her. The ferocious green eyes were unforgettable, the long pointed nose almost hiding the small mouth, now pursed in a tender smile, the piles of frizzy, strawlike hair. But where he had seen the woman before, he could not imagine. The woman beckoned coyly, and Francis went to her. Once they started dancing Francis had to fight for breath, they were whirling so rapidly in the dust. But he could not ask her to stop, she seemed so refined and enveloping, even if her body gave out a strong goaty odor.

"What a charming little boy you are," she remarked, doing a double turn. Her voice was a quiet singing voice but was quite clear above the creaking musicians. "And how nicely you dance—here, hold my left breast, please."

Francis obeyed, despite a faint nausea. "You see, I am really an aristocrat. You've obviously heard of the Marquis de Pfadade?"

"No," said Francis breathlessly.

"He is my father." She smiled, taking a great leap into the air, exposing a pair of muscular legs. "I am his only daughter, Pfoebe."

When they had finished dancing she drew Francis into the shadow of a tree and kept on smiling enigmatically. Under a lamp twinkling nearby a hoard of ephemeras danced away their one hysterical day. Francis was panting like a spent horse.

"Poor little boy is tired," Pfoebe said, stroking Francis's cheek with a loose and graceful gesture. "You and your distinguished uncle must come visit me." She gave a little titter. "And here is my address." It was written in mauve ink. "Now I really must go home—I have such a lot of studying to do."

"Don't go," said Francis suddenly, his voice returning. "Come and have a drink and meet Uncle—ah, but you know him?"

"Not personally," she answered coyly. "But naturally I know his name."

"Then do come and have a drink."

"No no. You don't really want me!"

"Of course I do," said Francis, uncomfortable in front of her piercing little eyes. "I wouldn't have asked you otherwise." He felt he did not really like Pfoebe, yet could not drag himself away.

"No I don't think I'll come." He did not know if there was not a slight bitterness in Pfoebe's smile, which seemed permanent.

"Well let me see you to your car."

"Ah no, dear little fellow."

"Then we will come visit you?" he said, with certain misgivings.

"Yes," Pfoebe said, winding her arm around his neck. "Do do come. I think you had better promise. Now will you promise? And bring your uncle."

"I promise," said Francis, longing to get loose.

"That's right. Good night, my little darling poo poo." Pfoebe kissed him lightly on his nose and skipped off on big padding feet, singing sadly as she went. A little later, he thought he heard a horse galloping away over the bridge of Saint-Roc.

Uncle Ubriaco had been looking for him and seemed a little short-tempered.

"Who's your lady friend?" he asked. "Do you know you've been gone for three hours?"

"Have you ever seen her before?" asked Francis. "I felt I had."

"Never!" replied Uncle Ubriaco shortly. "She looked terrifying. Who is she?"

Francis explained.

"Well, you looked pretty funny frolicking around the ring, all madame la Marquise and nearly no Francis. It's bedtime now."

The people were beginning to clear off, leaving a sea of litter behind them.

They took a swim in the pool before going to bed. Uncle Ubriaco was rather silent, and it took Francis some time to get to sleep that night, for he was listening to the noises outside. When he did eventually fall asleep, the stones got up and spoke to a group of dead hedgehogs and a solitary magpie. "The time has come," said a hunk of granite, "that the position be dragged to a logical conclusion."

"Dragged, whipped, or battered," added a hedgehog, drily. "As the case may be."

"Here come the servants," said the magpie.

"I stand for sorrow. Hold my hat boys, we're off." A line of blue maidservants in military formation got up out of the river.

"If Pfoebe could only join in," said a little bit of marble. "Now what in Hell is she doing?"

"Studying her pamphlets," said the hedgehog.

"Hammering away at her damned pamphlets. She's rather a bore, really."

"I stand for sorrow," repeated the hedgehog aggressively, "and the theory of the whole thing is logic. Pure insufferable mathematical logic, though it has *assets*. The time is coming when we shall claim our own (I worked that out by square root)."

"We'll start with the Lord's Prayer," said the granite. "And take the blessed Hemispheres as they come." Everybody laughed. "Now where's the Bishop?"

Francis saw himself hurrying towards the group, holding up his long purple robe with one hand and carrying in the other a huge breviary. His mitre was awry and he had a troubled frown. "Excuse me, brethren," he said, breathlessly straightening his mitre and mopping his forehead. "I was detained at an extreme unction." There was a mumbled greeting and a bit of calcareous rock got the giggles. "Now," he said severely, placing a pince-nez near the end of his nose, "let us hear the opening hymn, 'Faith of our fathers, holy faith,' etc."

He cleaned his teeth as they sang, beating time with one foot.

"Stop," he said, flinging his toothbrush into the river. "That will do. I will start with an SOS. Will Mrs. James Jeffery (not been heard of for two hundred years B.C.) please go straight back to Saint George's Hospital and claim one hundred pounds remittance." He paused as his face got enveloped in a small thundercloud of white flies. "And please treat me nicely," he added, emerging rather pale. "I don't think I can stand what's going to happen."

The congregation murmured amongst themselves, and the most dead of all the hedgehogs rose to his feet as spokesman. He coughed and cleared the grimy hairs out of his eyes.

"It's heartbreaking," he began in a monotonous voice, "but it's a matter of long nails. All the great of this world (amen) cannot help Your Lordship."

A look of sick depression twisted Francis's face. "But I thought," he said brokenly, "if one had the courage—"

"Courage," said the hedgehog, concealing a smile behind his claw, "is a doubtful virtue. You should kick and scream and cry and behave generally hysterically. Besides, you are not touching, you know."

"I know," said Francis turning away with a lump in his throat.

"You were made to stand square on your feet," continued the hedgehog relentlessly. "You're too resourceful."

"I know," said Francis again.

"You're harsh. You know fate really means nothing, you know about Nothing and the terrible imbecility of destiny."

"Ah yes. I know." By this time a stream of cold tears ran down each cheek, but nobody paid much attention. He looked lonely and small in his enormous purple robe. "Couldn't somebody for God's sake hold my hand?" he asked, looking around. They all looked negative and embarrassed. "All right, forget it. One, two, three for our Indian Lancers!"

They all started dancing and Francis hopped up and down, shouting and laughing, but his eyes looked frightened and unhappy.

At six in the morning the sun hit the top of the tent, awaking Francis and Uncle Ubriaco.

They had to lie in the pool to get cool, till the shadow of the cliff reached far enough for them to emerge.

"We've been here for a time now and not taken a single bicycle trip," said Ubriaco, completely concealed by water save his nose and mouth, "and Roger and Mabel have had no exercise at all. It's not good for them."

"I think that's a good idea," replied Francis. "Why don't we pay a visit to Pfoebe?"

"Yes," said Uncle Ubriaco. "We could do that. Go get the map."

Pfoebe lived up in the mountains where—according to the peasants—the thunderstorms came from to swell the river to miraculous dimensions. Her particular mountain was called Piedbrûlé, the Burnt Foot.

"If we started in half an hour," said Uncle Ubriaco, "we could get there by teatime. It's a difficult route, but it will be cooler up there." He ran his fingernail reflectively from Saint-Roc to Oeufmorte and on to Piedbrûlé. He was naked but for a green fishing hat decorated with salmon flies. Francis felt slightly sad as he watched him: he felt he would never love anybody so much as Uncle Ubriaco.

"There," said Ubriaco, indicating Oeufmorte, "we can have lunch. Apparently one eats well." Francis scarcely heard what he said. "We must oil the bicycles and fill the lamps. I suppose we must also get dressed. Now I must go and darn my trousers." Francis continued to sit, paring his toenails dreamily. Ubriaco was swearing quietly in the tent, bothered by the flies.

Three quarters of an hour later they left the village in commendable style, followed by dogs, children, stones, and general appreciation. The first part of the journey was almost unbearably hot, but towards lunchtime they started climbing the higher mountains. Great black thunderclouds rolled up behind the mountains and growled between distant rocks. Oeufmorte was one house and a barn; a rook sat screaming on the roof. The wind was cold and rattled the windows. They ate game for lunch, and Francis upset a whole bottle of red wine on Uncle Ubriaco, who accused him of doing it on purpose.

The other three people at lunch looked exactly alike, down to their black hats and the size of their huge black moustaches. They exchanged not a word, only glaring at each other and Francis, and pausing now and then to kick a pair of dogs who were busily tearing each other to bits under the table. The room was soon spattered with blood but nobody cared, and the cheese was brought in by the *patronne*, who looked like a medieval executioner. "Finished?" she said savagely. "Well, here's the fruit." She menaced Uncle Ubriaco with a goat's cheese and a little wizened bunch of grapes. "And now I'll bring you the bill."

They were fairly robbed but hurried out without argument. Francis caught a glimpse of three dark faces and three moustaches pressed to the window furtively as they departed.

The further they went, the more hostile became the landscape. Trees grew bony, and the rocks craggy and monstrous. All the birds were black, and their voices seemed hard as they stood despondently on scabs of grass or loped through the air. The road was a thin, lumpy rag trickling up into the mountains. Hardly a living soul was to be seen, and those they did see regarded them with such hate that they were obliged to quicken their pace.

Towards four o'clock they were halfway up Piedbrûlé. In a hollow at the summit they came upon the farm of the Marquis. It was dark and scorched by weather. There was a large greyish field behind the farmhouse. A horse was galloping round; a figure easily recognized as Pfoebe Pfadade stood upright on his back, cracking a long whip. She wore a little military jacket and nothing else at all. She was far too absorbed in her sport to notice the approach of Francis and Uncle Ubriaco. Around and around she thundered, throwing hunting cries and abuse at the already maddened horse, who gave a sort of shriek every time the whip made a weal on his belly.

They got to the gate of the field before Pfoebe wrenched her horse to a standstill. He was quaking and foaming all over and bleeding in several places.

"There's a good little chap," said Pfoebe, patting him kindly. "I'm very fond of dumb beasts," she explained, and leant towards Uncle Ubriaco confidentially. "I've heard such a lot about you, I felt we were fated to meet."

Uncle Ubriaco seemed to recoil into himself.

"It's funny how fate works," she continued, linking her arm through his and drawing him away from Francis. "We two have known each other a long long time." Uncle Ubriaco muttered something polite and stared straight ahead.

"I felt," she said, "what a great deal could come from a friendship between us. A friendship," she said, cocking her head on one side and smiling archly, "as a friendship between men. Two souls who understand each other. Two beings who speak the same language. Don't you think it is rather beautiful? Beautiful in a hard clean way?" Uncle Ubriaco muttered again and glanced back towards Francis, who was following at a dejected distance.

"Who knows," said Pfoebe, conducting them through a barn filled with sheep and rabbits in cages, "if there is not an astral connection between our planets?" They entered a dimly lit passage at the end of which a light could be seen through the crack in a door.

Pfoebe led the way into the room where an old gentleman of amazing distinction was sitting. He was poring over a large leather volume and let them get well into the room before he gave a great start and rose to his feet with a hundred apologies. "You understand, my dear sir, that I get so absorbed in my studies! I am most ravished to make your acquaintance, sir; and this surely is your delightful young friend?

"Let me offer you a little refreshment. Though," he said with a deprecating smile, "I cannot produce your golden English whiskey, I do have a little vintage sherry—a sherry . . . well sir, you shall see for yourself. The little boy shall have a taste too. They say that in England one cultivates a palate early, ha ha." He waved Pfoebe, who was still naked, over to the cupboard. She chose a dusty black bottle and four glasses which appeared slightly unwashed. The Marquis extracted the cork with infinite care and poured each a quarter glass of the liquid.

"To your health," said the Marquis, flourishing his glass towards the ceiling, "and your good luck, not to mention your courage in visiting a lonely old gentleman in his hermitage." Very delicately he sipped and raised his eyes for a fraction of a second. "Ah! the same mellow draught," he murmured. "You sir," he said, laying his hand on Uncle Ubriaco's shoulder, "have no doubt a passion for first editions too?"

"It depends what's in them," answered Uncle Ubriaco. "I've met first editions that made me feel ill."

"Ah volumes, volumes," said the old gentleman ecstatically. "The thrill to touch the leather weathered by the years and the bronzed pages blessed by reverend fingers! I have a little collection, sir, which would no doubt interest you. Now let me see." He hurried over to a glass-faced bookcase that looked as if it had not been opened for generations. "Ah, dear friends," he said, addressing a row of expressionless-looking books, "how I lean upon you in my solitude!" He drew out two brown leather volumes. "These," he said, stroking the covers, "are genuine first editions signed by the author."

In two hours' time three spindle-legged tables were piled high with books of all sizes. Ubriaco was reaching a point of exasperation when Pfoebe announced dinner.

The dining room was one of the coldest rooms they'd ever entered. The ancient casement leaked draughts and made the candles shudder. But the Marquis and his daughter appeared immune to the cold. He talked and talked with ever-increasing volubility over a lukewarm meal consisting of a shallow pool of soup each, one potato, and a small square of cheese, which the guests were obliged to refuse owing to the obvious impossibility of it surviving a complete circulation. After much careful study, explained the Marquis, he had concluded that a vegetarian diet was the only salvation of the human race.

After dinner Francis and Uncle Ubriaco were shown up to their rooms and left. Both rooms were much the same temperature as the dining room, but it was too late to return to Saint-Roc that night. "To avoid freezing to death," remarked Uncle Ubriaco, "we will probably be obliged to do gymnastic exercises all night. That," he continued, warming to his subject, "was the most scandalous meal I was ever insulted with. And now I suppose for the sake of keeping the little life we have left in our bodies we must go down and support that gibbering old monkey and his monstrous daughter, by the only fire in the house, till we go to bed and die of exposure."

They groped their way down the stairs, which were plunged in pitch darkness, and felt for the door. Uncle Ubriaco imagined he had found the right place and turned a knob which let them into the wrong room: a huge kitchen with a magnificent roaring fire and an immense oven giving out a smell of roasting meat. They gazed around astonished. Pewter plates decorated the walls and the ceiling was hung with plentiful provisions of ham, joints, and clusters of sausages. They basked in the warmth for a second or two and then Uncle Ubriaco opened the first cupboard he came to. Within was a curious collection: rows upon rows of small curved bones polished white and standing erect, each in a bracket and bearing a small ticket tied onto the other end. APRIL 2ND A.D. 1890. BENEDICTUS DEI. JUNE 19TH A.D. 1900. BENEDICTUS DITTO. et cetera. They amounted to thousands. Uncle Ubriaco and Francis stood before the open cupboard in wondering contemplation till the distant sound of an opening door roused them to action. Uncle Ubriaco closed the cupboard and they slipped quickly and quietly back into the freezing, dark passage. "I feel we shall see that kitchen again before the night is out," whispered Ubriaco as Francis collided with Pfoebe. She had come upon them without a sound.

"My dear! I am so sorry!" she said in her soft singsong. "But I felt you might not find your way to the parlor so I came to help you." She found Uncle Ubriaco in the dark and took a swift snap at his ear. He winced with pain. "Father is preparing some card tricks."

The card tricks lasted a long time; they were of immense intricacy. The bronze clock struck eleven before Pfoebe suddenly suggested a walk, cutting the Marquis short in a new trick. "That's right, a breath of fresh air before bed," he said heartily, unwillingly parted from his two packs of cards. "I always used to take a breather at this time before I got my chest trouble." He gave a short explanatory cough. "Well I will bid you a good night sir, and to you, little chap. That's right, a good British handshake!"

Outside a high wind was blowing, and a spattering rain. The moon appeared now and again, ghostly between watery black clouds. Pfoebe took Uncle Ubriaco and Francis by the arm and drew them along with terrific speed and force. They seemed to go quite a long way before the sound of roaring water became audible. Soon they found themselves standing on the edge of a rock, gazing dizzily down into a seething river that foamed and roared.

"Now how about a swim?" She laughed.

Uncle Ubriaco gave a sort of laugh between his chattering teeth, but Pfoebe had stripped off her military jacket and poised herself completely naked on the edge. Then she took a leap into the sinister chasm and was lost in the blackness.

"Good God. Suicide," said Francis. "I don't see why we had to be brought into it."

"I'm not going down to recover the body anyhow," said Uncle Ubriaco, peering over the edge where nothing was to be seen. "The body will probably be outside our tent tomorrow morning." They listened fearfully to the terrible noise of the river, then from below rang out a girlish "Cooo ee."

They exchanged glances.

"Aren't you coming in boys, the water is lovely!" A bit later Pfoebe appeared above the rock, which she had mounted by some mysterious means; before Uncle Ubriaco could protect himself he was crushed against her dripping body and whirling in a wild dance perilously near the precipice. All the birds awakened and set to a mad chorus of screams, flitting back and forth across the sky. The night seemed to burst open. Then, as suddenly as she had begun she ceased, flinging Uncle Ubriaco yards away with one hand. "That was fun." She laughed, helping him up maternally. "And so to bed." She set off at triple gallop.

Once everybody seemed to be well out of the way and safely in bed, Uncle Ubriaco stole to Francis's room, where he found him fully dressed and in bed.

"We're going to visit that kitchen," he whispered. "I've never been so hungry in my life. Take off your shoes." They found the door of the kitchen and opened it without a sound. There sat the Marquis with his back to them, at his side a dish of mutton chops. He did not hear them enter. "That," whispered Ubriaco savagely, "explains the museum pieces. Bloody hell," he continued, shutting the door.

The vines of Saint-Roc were ripening, and the peasants were cursing the heat and lack of rain. But the country was rich. Day after day Francis and Uncle Ubriaco basked in the sun, told stories, and swam. In the evening Francis learned how to play Russian billiards and boule. They drank quantities of burning white marc. They went to a bullfight and visited some caves. Otherwise they did not move much out of Saint-Roc.

"Yes," replied Ubriaco to Francis's question as they were sitting outside the tent one morning that dawned strange and dead. "I appeared in the great war, though I did try and get out of it."

The flies seemed to be bloated and unable to fly more than a few yards without dropping to the ground.

"I was with a man named Ulrich Weg. He begged me to cross the border into Switzerland but I missed the last train. Ulrich got safely into Switzerland and I was left behind. He told me afterwards how he managed to get past the army doctor; I never thought he would manage that, being one of the fittest people I ever met—excluding your friend la Marquise."

"What did he do?" said Francis, feeling himself on dangerous ground.

"Well, he came into the office with no trousers on and said, 'Guten Tag, guten Tag, Herr Doktor.' Then when asked to write his residence, nationality, name, name of parents, age, and finally date of birth, he wrote 1914 to every question, added up the result, and presented the answer to the doctor. He was let into Switzerland as a harmless lunatic.

"I, on the other hand, whiled away four years in a German concentration camp. So Ulrich's story is the only war souvenir I know."

Then, when they were marching in the village, a thunderstorm burst and down came the rain in torrents, tearing the grapes off the vines and rushing through the square in streams.

"The river might rise tonight," said Rosaline. "You would do well to clear away your tent or else you and the tent might be in Marseilles tomorrow morning."

"Do they know if it's going to rise?"

"I can't say, it depends on the rain in the mountains."

"That's the *sacrés* Pfadades who've sent us this," said Uncle Ubriaco bitterly.

It rained till dark and then the moon came out. A peasant, Noël, took them in a boat to the tent: it was squashed flat. On the way Francis thought he saw a little white cat walking about underwater.

Simon helped them to carry their things from the boat to the Café Pirigou, where they installed themselves once more. They never went back to the tent—the thunderstorm marked the day.

The following morning the sun came out as hot as

ever and the river had hardly risen at all; only piles of crushed grapes under the vines told of the storm. That morning Francis had his first quarrel with Ubriaco. It came after a telephoned telegram. Uncle Ubriaco disappeared into the Hôtel du Centre and came back without a word. Now in Saint-Roc a telephone call was an event, so Francis said, "Oh, who was that?"

"Nothing," said Ubriaco shortly, shifting a bit of blue paper in his pocket.

"How do you mean, nothing?"

"You're very curious, aren't you?"

"I was interested, that's all," said Francis. "Of course, if it's private—"

"Well if you must know, it was Amelia. So there."

Francis jerked upright. "But then she knows where we are. Oh hell."

"No, she doesn't. I've had three like this already. I gave her a poste restante address at Chavaltras. The telegrams are sent on from there."

"She'll know soon, then. Oh damn. You didn't tell me anything about this."

"I thought you'd make a scene."

"A scene?" said Francis angrily. "When the devil have I ever made a scene? God Almighty, that's a dirty thing to say."

"You're making one now anyhow," replied Uncle Ubriaco. Francis threw a bit of bread on the floor and left the room. Furious, he walked down to the river where his anger cooled, leaving him in a state of misery. When he went back, he found Ubriaco with icicles hanging out of his mouth.

"Well," said Francis into the silence. "Well."

"You don't trust me," said Uncle Ubriaco.

"No I don't," said Francis, fiddling.

"Ha," said Uncle Ubriaco.

"I didn't mean that exactly," said Francis, floundering. "What I meant was I think at times you do silly things."

"Let me run my affairs myself."

"Naturally, it's not my business," answered Francis, getting angry again. "Naturally, it has nothing whatever to do with me."

"It has in a way. But I think I am old enough to run things for myself my own way."

"You've not been very efficient up till now," said Francis, wondering how it was going to end.

"That," said Ubriaco, "is my business."

"Oh, let's stop this," said Francis.

"It's you who're going on."

"That's a lie."

"Oh I'm a liar, am I? Thank you."

"No, not a liar, but sometimes you forget what's gone before, and imagine the rest."

"Will you kindly stop insisting on this painful conversation?"

"I'm not enjoying it at all."

"One would imagine you were."

"Let's go for a walk," said Francis desperately.

All through the walk Uncle Ubriaco preserved a stony silence. Then Francis started feeling guilty, and that he would do anything to make Ubriaco talk.

The next morning Ubriaco seemed as if nothing at all had happened. A man with a drum was marching around the square, banging and shouting—"Ladies and gentlemen, tonight is the night you are to be presented the world-famous Tom Angadi, the Great Indian Kafir, and his medium, Olga. Tickets one franc apiece. Performance at nine o'clock on the terrace of the Hôtel du Centre. Mysterious! Breathtaking! Dramatic!" Judging from his long curls and emotional voice, the drummer was presumably Tom Angadi himself, the famous Kafir. "I wonder if the Kafir can really produce spirits," said Ubriaco.

"I hope not," said Francis. "I'm pretty certain they would come straight after me. I seem to attract ghosts like a cheese attracts maggots. When I was in the nursery there was an awful old dame who used to chase me around pillar-boxes. And another like a black bird with a long neck, who used to come rising out of the sink when I wanted to wash my hands. But the worst one was the tree boy. He used to appear in the monkey puzzle tree that grew outside the night nursery. Not often but quite often enough at night. I used to look out and there he sat high up on one of the top branches, with no clothes on.

"I was terrified, and nobody ever believed me when I told them about him."

At 8:30 the Kafir and his medium installed a mechanical piano and a lot of sacks to obscure the view from vulgar peepers; at 9:00 the terrace at la Marie's was stocked with a good audience. The Kafir's performance was slow and unoriginal. Francis and Uncle Ubriaco saw most of the show by moving a sack about half a foot. Tom Angadi the Great Indian Kafir did a bit of phony mesmerising (*Vous dormez, Vous dormez*) and one or two Old World conjuring tricks while the mechanical piano did its best.

"I think we could do better ourselves," said Uncle Ubriaco. "Tomorrow we'll give a rival performance chez Rosaline."

Rosaline was charmed. "We'll make money on the drinks!" she exclaimed. "And we'll make Simon act too! He and Francis can make a dwarf: Simon will be the head and feet and Francis the arms."

"A very good opening number," said Uncle Ubriaco. "I shall be the *Cafard*, I'll dye my hair and face blue."

Early in the morning they got to work on the posters: GRANDE SOIRÉE DU CAFARD HINDOU. THE GREAT EVENING OF THE HINDU COCKROACH. FREE ENTRY EASY EXIT. DRINKING COMPULSORY.

They set it up on Rosaline's terrace. After breakfast they rode into Pontfantôme, the local marketing town, and bought all they needed. Somebody lent them a gramophone. When they got back for lunch Pfoebe was waiting for them.

"The dwarf's head," exclaimed Uncle Ubriaco when he had got over the first shock. "Pfoebe will make a marvellous dwarf's head!"

"I shall do a number on my own," proclaimed Pfoebe mysteriously. "A surprise number." She was full of ideas and rather retarded the operations.

They prepared the program, which went as follows—

1. Miraculous Dwarf Growing (Maître Cafard, Master Cockroach)
2. Miraculous Bullfight
3. Miraculous Cure
4. Mesmerising of the Wild Panther
   INTERVAL
5. Jiggery Pokery MacFoozle
6. Surprise Number
7. Finale of a generally miraculous nature

By eight o'clock all was ready. Uncle Ubriaco was dressed in a long red robe like a cardinal, while his face, hands, and hair were dyed bright blue. Pfoebe sat in the kitchen ready to do the Dwarf while Francis cried out from the veranda. Soon the café was crowded out. Uncle Ubriaco gave a sinister speech while Francis rushed around to the back door to do the Dwarf's arms. The Dwarf appeared, on a table in front of the curtains that separated the kitchen from the café. There was wild applause all around. Francis let off a firework, made a few incantations, and rapped Pfoebe soundly on the head with her magic wand, whereupon the Dwarf grew to full size and there was more wild applause.

Next came the bullfight, with Uncle Ubriaco (Master Cockroach) and Pfoebe dressed as a bull. She gave a terrifying performance and nearly disemboweled Ubriaco before he at last managed to hypnotize her into a slow gavotte.

Francis and Uncle Ubriaco took the next number, the Miraculous Cure. Francis had to come in dressed in a sheet, holding a huge stomach and say "Sir, I am ill, ohhh." Whereupon Ubriaco hid him on the table and cut a huge incision in the stomach. (Moans from Francis.) Ubriaco then plunged in his hand and drew forth alarm clocks, shoes, sausages (which he smelt, licked, and ate), nails, hammers, tomatoes, mule chains, an oil lamp, and paper trailers. Francis then jumped lightly from the table and pronounced himself miraculously cured. Applause and catcalls from the audence.

Pfoebe came on again in the Panther Act, which finished successfully, apart from a slight mauling of Ubriaco's left hand.

After the interval, once they managed to call order, all three took the Jiggery Pokery MacFoozle: Francis lay a quantity of pot eggs to the tune of *"Ange du Paradis"* and gibberish from Uncle Ubriaco, while Pfoebe sang the text and milked horse sausages out of the gramophone.

Then they were ready for the Surprise Act. Pfoebe disappeared into the recesses of the kitchen. "When I whistle," she told Francis, "I'm ready for my entry. Put on a polka before I come in." They waited for ten minutes in trepidation for Pfoebe's surprise, Uncle Ubriaco assiduously entertaining the audience while sweat ran down his blue face. Then a piercing whistle blared from the kitchen. Francis put on the polka, and they stood aside. Pfoebe parted the curtains with a flourish and entered in a black corset and tall boots, leading a furious billy goat. The audience was petrified. A satanic dance then began. The goat reared on his hind legs, appearing at once angry and terrified of his partner. They darted and plunged and performed the most amazing contortions in a sort of polka, more and more quickly till it was difficult to distinguish which was the goat and which was Pfoebe. It might have gone on still had the goat not leapt towards the gramophone in a wild effort to escape. Pfoebe, goat, and gramophone all went flying and landed in a heap on top of the terrified audience. This unloosed the crowd. Bottles and hats hurtled round the room. Rosaline disappeared onto the veranda shrieking to Heaven and Hell for protection.

At that moment a respectable young man, the son of the village aristocrat, was just mounting the steps to the terrace. "Is there a certain Monsieur Ubriaco here?" he inquired politely. Rosaline jerked her thumb over her shoulder. He looked in on the turmoil in the café: a crowd of yelling peasants, a lady in a black corset, a maddened billy goat, and in the midst of it all a red-robed, gesticulating figure with a bright blue face.

"Mon Dieu! How is one to tell which is he?"

"By the blue face. But I wouldn't advise you to go in. I'm going to get a gendarme." The young man, however, pushed his way in, narrowly escaping getting brained as he approached Uncle Ubriaco. He took him by the arm and was rudely shaken off. "Monsieur, you are required on the telephone. A lady, your daughter, no doubt mistook our house for the *cabine téléphonique.* She is asking for you."

"Get away," shouted Uncle Ubriaco, fending off a flying beer bottle. "I'm not interested." The young man made a grateful and difficult retreat, escaping with only minor injuries.

Later on, however, when the café had emptied, leaving a chaos of broken bottles and overturned chairs, Uncle Ubriaco thought about the telephone call. Rosaline, Francis, and he were sitting on the only whole chairs, breathing heavily.

"Well, she knows where we are," said Francis. "What are we going to do?"

"We'll have to move tonight. She might be here tomorrow morning. You never know with Amelia."

"Did he say where the telephone call came from?"

"No. It might have come from anywhere between here and Paris."

"Don't go away," said Rosaline wiping her eyes. "I shall be so lonely!"

"We'll come back," said Uncle Ubriaco. Simon was wandering around the room fruitlessly, looking miserable.

"We'll leave most of our things here as a guarantee," said Ubriaco. "The tent and everything. Now, how much do you think tonight's damages will come to?"

"That's all right," said Rosaline. "I checked on everybody here, and I'll make them pay up. Where's the Marquise gone to?" Pfoebe and the goat had disappeared. "Don't worry about it, let's take one thing at a time."

Good-byes took place at four o'clock in the morning. Simon and Rosaline were weeping copiously in the wrecked café; Roger of Kildare and Darling Little Mabel were once more ready for the road. Uncle Ubriaco and Francis disengaged themselves from Rosaline's arms, promising faithfully to write often and return soon. They mounted the bicycles and pedalled out of Saint-Roc. Francis was singing, rather dejectedly—

Do you know my Aunt Eliza? Wha, ha, ha, ha, haa.
She is blue but don't despise her. Wha, ha, ha, ha, haa.
Now you'll excuse me laughing like I'm inclined to do—
But, do you know my Aunt Eliza? Wha ha, ha, ha, haa.

Uncle Ubriaco and Francis sat in the public gardens of Nîmes wondering what to do. "I liked Saint-Roc," said Ubriaco. "It's all a great nuisance." They were in front of an eighteenth-century monument writhing with unctuous reclining women and obese cherubs.

"This," said Ubriaco, "is the most beautiful public garden in the world. Now, what exactly are we going to do?"

"I can't say," said Francis, fanning himself with his hat. "But France is quite a big place. We might go and stay with somebody you know. You seem to know everybody anyhow."

Ubriaco pondered a bit. "That's a good idea, and I believe I have it! But he lives a long way off, somewhere in the region of Béziers."

"Who is he?"

"Jerome Jones. He's a shoemaker. He's always at home, because he's paralysed and can only move from the waist up. He's a charming man and will be delighted to see us."

Jerome Jones lived in the village of Sansnom. It was a lost, silent village with small and discreet streets overhung with vines and trees. In front of the fountain in the little square was Jerome Jones's shop. He sat on a mattress near a big low window, shaded by a tree outside. The room was whitewashed and without furniture, but hundreds of shoes and clogs stood in rows along the walls like patient ghosts. In the centre of the room grew a lemon tree, Jerome's great pride—he had brought it from Sicily before he got paralysed.

"I was thinking about you," he said to Uncle Ubriaco. "And I heard you coming."

He had a tall bald head, fringed with black hair, and a narrow ivory-coloured face, smooth and ageless.

"I have a lot to tell you, but first we must have lunch. As you see, I'm in very good health." They sat on the floor, and the old servant woman brought them quantities of baked potatoes with butter and salad, and an excellent white wine. Jerome drank water. "If you remember," he told Ubriaco, "I always used to be drunk, but since then I've managed to procure regular supplies of opium from a friend who goes to Marseilles every fortnight. It's far better than alcohol: the effect is gentle and lasting and I feel very well. I've almost become a teetotaler." He smiled.

"I'm anxious to hear what's been happening to you," said Ubriaco. "It seems a long time since I was here." The atmosphere of Jerome's room reminded Francis of the dusk. Even the little shop one traversed to enter Jerome's room seemed unvisited. And when one got to the room itself, which looked onto a damp green garden, it became hushed and still, and the light itself was greenish, like the light of an aquarium.

"I've had great need to see you and talk to you," answered Jerome, lighting a lamp for his opium pipe. He took a great gasp of smoke and continued talking, holding his breath and letting out a thin thread of smoke only very gradually.

"I scarcely see anyone nowadays. People are generally such imbeciles that I mostly prefer being alone. So you can imagine it's a great delight to see you. I smoke, dream, work, and eat a lot of preserved fruit. I adore preserved fruit," he added, opening a large wooden box filled with sugarplums. They took one each. "I have thought about you a great deal, Ubriaco, and really hungered to see you again. Tell me, how is Amelia?"

"Amelia," said Uncle Ubriaco, "becomes more Christian every day. She's almost impossible now. I havn't seen her for some time."

"I knew you had left her," said Jerome. "And I wasn't surprised. I never saw anyone change so much in seven years. The first time I saw her she was a delightful, gay little girl. Then later, after she'd been to that convent, she seemed to degenerate into an hysterical old woman. She must be about fourteen now? Even her face became dry and peaked. It's a great pity."

"Yes, she used to be charming," said Uncle Ubriaco. "When she was about seven years old."

"Adults are terrible people," said Jerome. "And nearly

everyone over the age of ten becomes petrified. Yet children can be very objectionable. One must ignore birthdays entirely, to be acceptable at all."

"You're out of danger here," said Uncle Ubriaco. "And I see you have no clock."

"No clocks at all," said Jerome. "And I make a point of never knowing either the date or day of the week. It must be nearly fifteen years since I saw a mirror. I have no idea what I look like. Old Valérie shaves me every morning and I know I'm going bald but that's all. I have no curiosity about my face. Accident has placed me apart from active life, so I enjoy the other as completely as I can."

He was cooking little balls of opium over his lamp and smoking them in a single, long breath. The smell was very sweet. "For the last three days," he continued, "I have been enjoying a dream that continues every night. It is very strange and I am most interested to see what is to happen. It commences with a pale green snowstorm in a countryside that is neither light nor dark. I seem to be drifting through the snow without difficulty, past trees whose branches are like ragged wings and drip on me as I pass. I am neither warm nor cold, and I cannot tell if I have any clothes on. I meet various people on the way whose presence is sharply defined though they have no faces. They are drifting in different directions in the same manner as myself. The country is unvaried and for a long distance I can see buildings, but sometimes on the way I meet bird cages—some of them empty, others have different shapes inside—also terracotta busts and statues dotted here and there and representing various things.

"My companion is a transparent globe that follows me closely wherever I go. It sings as we move along but I can hear no words, though the voice is quite clear. There's something unbearable about the singing of this transparent globe. Some time later we arrive at a monastery and are both cordially received by a number of monks with dogs' heads. They say they are bloodstock angels and this is the stable. We are led into an enormous cloister which surrounds a garden, where there are trees with fruit wandering all over the branches. It is still snowing. In the center of the garden a diamond-shaped pool lies, covered with ice. On the ice stands a young and beautiful girl made of terra-cotta, but she is not a statue like those outside. She is alive." He stopped. "That is as far as it goes."

In the following days at Sansnom Jerome seemed scarcely to live apart from his dream. Francis and Uncle Ubriaco were also drawn into his atmosphere, living in the immense calm of Jerome's room, listening to him talking and watching him smoke his opium. They very seldom went out into the village. Sometimes they sat naked in the stream that ran through the garden behind Jerome's house, then would return to his room, where he sat, eager to tell them what had passed during the night.

"I have met the terra-cotta girl," he explained. "It is still snowing, the terra-cotta girl comes to me and gives me a little purple violet. She says it is my marriage gift, we are to be wed."

Francis thought he saw an emerald green shade around Jerome's jaw but decided it must be a reflection from the garden outside.

They all became moody and lost more and more interest in the world outside Jerome's room. They almost ceased to sit in the stream in the garden, and never thought about meals or the day of the week, even forgetting to feel bored on Sundays.

They did not know how long they had been in Sansnom, but the sun was still very hot, so they supposed it was not yet winter. Francis, however, remembered to send a postcard to Rosaline saying they were in good health and wished to hear some news from Saint-Roc. A letter arrived from Rosaline by return of post.

Dear Friends,

I have plenty of news for you and am glad to have your address. Here is what I have to tell. A week ago when I returned from Pontfantôme la Marie says, "There's a telephone call for you from Paris. They will ring again at nine o'clock."

"I will be there," say I. At nine-fifteen I am called to the telephone box.

"Who is there?" say I.

"Mademoiselle Ubriaco! I want to speak to my father."

"He's gone."

"Has he left any luggage? Do you think he will return?"

"He left no luggage."

"Did he pay his bill?"

"He owes me nothing!"

"Had my father anybody with him?"

"A young gentleman and sometimes a lady."

"That's very unfortunate. Had my father good appetite?"

"Your father had very good appetite."

"Do you know where he has gone?"

"I am not permitted to say. You had better approach other people in the village. They may be able to tell you."

"Thank you. Good-bye."

"Good-bye, Mademoiselle." And I put down the receiver. Three days ago the curé comes to me and says he has received a letter from your daughter saying you are gallivanting around France with vulgar individuals and that it's the curé's duty to help find you. The curé says, "It's not our affair to mix in such things. The gentleman's helped you earn your bread."

"It is understood, Monsieur le Curé," I reply. I have since received a letter from your daughter and two telegrams, all much the same as our telephone conversation. You have no cause to make bad blood, she has no idea where you are, and I do not think she will come here, so you may return soon. I miss you both very much.

Simon and my mother send you a kiss.
Yours very affectionately
Your friend
Rosaline.

They read the letter twice, talked awhile, and forgot.

Jerome was sleeping later and later into the morning. Sometimes he did not awake till midday and went to bed at seven-thirty in the evening. His work was neglected. He increased the number of his opium pipes and seemed to suck in the smoke more avariciously than before.

"My best man has led me out into the snow once more; many people drift past playing bone flutes. The globe seems pleased and bounds gaily along. Away in the mountains, most of which are volcanoes, there seems to be a hunt taking place. Quite soon the quarry leaps across our path; it is a wolf. My best man cracks it on the head with his rosary beads and it dies instantly. He picks it up and slings it across his shoulders with a satisfied smile. 'The wedding breakfast,' he says."

Jerome was the next to receive a letter from Amelia. He tried hard to raise interest, but the effort seemed too much for him. He put the letter into Ubriaco's hand and with that seemed to return into his own thoughts. The letter said Amelia intended to come visit Jerome, "knowing his wisdom, and that she would pray him for advice in this heartbreaking matter." For the first time in many days Ubriaco and Francis walked out into the village square to think. There was something startling in being once more in the full glare of the sun. "I feel like a mushroom," said Francis, "that has grown in the dark."

"We must say good-bye to Jerome," said Ubriaco, pleasantly conscious of the warmth outside: Jerome's room, on reflection, seemed chilly and dark.

When they told Jerome they must leave, he nodded and said he would try to calm Amelia. It seemed an effort for him to talk, and when they took their leave, Francis thought he seemed to become misty.

They made towards the mountains of the Lozère, in the direction of Saint-Roc. They journeyed through sad red country, where the weather broke; they climbed a high mountain where the road was perpendicular, and far away on the summit they reached a plateau where all the trees were bleached and leafless. It was a flat silvery plain, lifeless. Then they descended perilously upon a small town lying amongst well-wooded mountains. They stayed one night and set off next day. After several days' journey they chose a village divided in two by the River Lozère. The weather was cold. The people seemed hostile as in Pfoebe's country, brutalized by scratching at their miserable soil.

There was nothing much to do except go for walks. Sometimes they climbed along the big stones in the river's bed; other times they climbed to the rocky tops of neighbouring mountains, where Uncle Ubriaco talked about astronomy. He found Francis very ignorant indeed and took a long time disillusioning him about the moon: Francis had always thought it swelled and decreased in actual fact. They saw a lot of different-colored grasshoppers—blue, green, and red, an adder, a buzzard. Uncle Ubriaco explained that mushrooms were much the same substance as the whites of egg. Since Francis didn't like eggs, he was rather put off mushrooms. Ubriaco seemed to be carrying a weight, and when he was not enlightening Francis about the devious ways of nature, he was silent and preoccupied. He had also caught a bad cold and often spoke longingly of the sun at Saint-Roc, which would still be shining.

During Ubriaco's long silences Francis would amuse himself by looking back at the brighter periods of his life spent at Crackwood. They were not many. He remembered skating on a lake north of Crackwood one hard winter and afterwards getting drunk on mulled ale with Pretty, the chauffeur. He could still smell the pub and see the huge tureen of mulled ale bubbling with spice on the oven. He remembered the roasting apples floating in the ale and the sticks of cinnamon, and how, after he was well inebriated, he had tried to show Pretty a red-haired man walking through the snow carrying two baskets of summer flowers. He remembered first refusing to go to church, and the scene outside the lavatory with his mother. He remembered being sick on the tennis court before a whole party of local people and being requested to leave the hunt ball. The smell of sandalwood in the ivory workbox, the lies he told when he was late for dinner. He would muse and watch Ubriaco out of the corner of his eye.

One day Ubriaco said, "I can't stand this place any longer."

"Well, let's go," said Francis.

"It would be the same," he replied moodily.

"We might go back to Saint-Roc?"

So they left for Saint-Roc in a rainstorm.

Rosaline was overjoyed and the weather was warm. "Last evening," said Rosaline, "I saw a spider in your bedroom. That means hope. *Araignée le soir: espoir. Araignée le matin: chagrin.* I knew then you'd return."

They walked down to the mushroom rock and took

a swim. Simon was in the café to welcome them when they got in. It rained a little during the night, so the next day they went out to look for snails. The river had risen somewhat. "Don't take snails from the cemetery," warned Rosaline, "or I shall refuse to cook them. But you will find plenty on the little wall that runs along Noël's vineyard."

They picked about three or four dozen snails.

"You starve them for three days," said Uncle Ubriaco, "and then wash them in vinegar and salt water. That makes them vomit so they're clean for cooking. Then you boil them and make garlic sauce. They're delicious."

"There'll be plenty for us three," said Rosaline, poking a large snail in his soft green body. "We can put them in the clothes basket with a tray on top. I shan't be washing much now as the river's getting cold."

Francis awoke early in the morning. Uncle Ubriaco was still sleeping. He watched a spider spinning down from the ceiling and dangling in the sunlight that came in from the shutters. He tried to remember Rosaline's proverb: *Araignée le matin, araignée le matin*; Spider in the morning, mourning, he said to himself; spider at night, delight.

A very soft knock came on the door. It was Rosaline. "Your daughter," she whispered in great agitation, "is here. She wanted to bring you up your café au lait, but I would not permit it."

"Damn," said Uncle Ubriaco savagely. "I had better go down and see her."

Francis was alone for three hours. Every time the clock struck he said, "Hear it not, Duncan, for it is a knell / That summons thee to Heaven or to Hell." As the clock struck the quarter as well as the half hour and the hour, he got irritated with repeating himself but found he couldn't stop.

Rosaline appeared at intervals with the bulletin.

"They kissed each other on sight. He said, 'What are you doing here, Amelia?' but didn't seem angry." Or else, "They've gone walking down by the river arm in arm; it doesn't look good for you." Francis nearly went mad. At last Ubriaco returned. "She seems calm enough," he said, "but doesn't want to see you."

"What are you going to do?" said Francis.

"I shall have to take her off," he explained. "She promised me that if I stay with her for only three days that is all she asks. I shall have to go. I'll take her to an aunt at Valence and come back."

"Put her on a train," said Francis.

"No, I can't do that," said Uncle Ubriaco.

"You'll never come back," said Francis.

"Of course I will."

"Don't be more of a fool than you can help."

"Didn't I say I can run my own affairs?"

"If you go you won't find me waiting here. I'm off."

"You can't do that."

"Your daughter is asking for you downstairs," said Rosaline, popping in.

"You must trust me and wait here," said Ubriaco.

"No."

"Try to understand, can't you?"

"Stop shaking me, my teeth will drop out."

"Francis, don't be pigheaded."

"Do you take me for an imbecile?"

"No. Please understand."

"Understand!"

"Yes, and wait for me—only three days and I'll be back, little Francis."

"Don't talk to me as if I'm a doorknob. I'm going if you do—in the other direction. When you've arranged your genital responsibilities so that life is bearable to you I'll come see you."

"But what will you do?"

"That's my business," said Francis, wondering miserably if he could get a job as a concierge or lavatory attendant.

"No you've got to wait for me. You must!"

"Oh clear out and leave me alone."

"I'll come back anyhow in three days."

Uncle Ubriaco left, his coat still hanging in the room. Francis stared at it as if trying to hypnotize it off the hook. Rosaline came in weeping.

"He's such a weak man," she said.

"Help me pack."

"What are you going to do?"

"I'm going."

"What! and leave us, oh no."

"I shall be sorry to leave you, but I'm going."

"A little boy like you all alone. Why it's monstrous!"

"Yes a poor little boy all alone in the big big world."

"No Francis, I shall not permit you to go. Anyhow for three days. Ubriaco will come back."

"And I'm the Lady of Shalott in the meantime? Oh no."

He was stuffing a pillowcase with possessions. His fingers were stone cold; Rosaline stood by, weeping and wringing her hands.

"There!" said Francis. "Now we'll go down and get drunk."

He sat in the kitchen with the old woman and Tante Gabrielle, huge and deaf, and drank a tumbler of marc. "And he left poor little Francis all alone!" said Rosaline, going through all the details. "And look at him now, getting drunk!"

Francis accosted the wine merchant and got the promise of a lift to Orange, where he could take a train to Paris the same night.

The Pirigou family did all they could through prayer and threat to prevent him going, but Francis was unshakable.

The wine merchant left him at the station in Orange at four in the afternoon.

"The *rapide* doesn't leave till nine-thirty this evening," said the clerk. Francis deposited his pillowcase and walked into town, drank four black coffees, bought a book, and walked in the public garden. Time did not move. Francis found he could not read, and the evening was cold. He went back into town and tried to get run over. Failing in this, he went and bought a packet of cigarettes, walked to the Roman Arena and found he hadn't the heart to go in. He bought a newspaper and threw it away immediately. He tried kicking himself on the shins to see if it would hurt, and it did. He wanted to meet Lucrezia Borgia and get poisoned. The thought of food made him sick. He went into a café and telephoned Rosaline. He cried down the telephone to the edification of two drinkers of Byrrh cassis.

"Don't go tonight," said Rosaline.

"Stay till tomorrow."

"Well, just till tomorrow," said Francis.

"Stay in Orange," suggested Rosaline, "and tell me your telephone number so I can ring you up tomorrow morning if there's any news."

"I'll ring you again this evening when I know where I'm staying."

The patron of the café found him a hotel and he telephoned Rosaline again, telling her carefully where he could be found. He went to bed at nine o'clock, didn't sleep at all, got up at seven, drank two black coffees and went for a walk. When the shops opened he bought a bottle of *fine* and a bunch of grapes and returned to his room. The morning seemed as if it would never end. Francis counted the rooftops and tried to get drunk. At eleven he was called to the telephone. He could hardly talk, his mouth was so sore with smoking. It was Rosaline. Apparently Uncle Ubriaco had telephoned. "I told him," said Rosaline, "that you had gone. I gave him your telephone number and said that you were in Orange but that tonight if you heard nothing you'd be gone, probably to America or China to take up the white slave traffic. He said he would telephone you immediately."

All morning Francis waited. He told all the waiters where he would be if he was wanted on the telephone. Nothing happened. He drank two black coffees for lunch, noted with satisfaction that his face looked pale and wild in the mirror. In the afternoon he drank more fine and tried to go to sleep. Still nothing happened. At three-thirty he ordered a taxi, told all the waiters his name in case somebody called Uncle Ubriaco telephoned, that he had left for Saint-Roc and not America, that he had waited four hours for the call that never came. Then he got into the taxi and returned to Saint-Roc.

"I don't understand at all," said Rosaline. "He seemed so urgent to know where you were. I hope nothing terrible has happened. People in the village say she had a revolver."

"I don't believe it," said Francis angrily.

"You look like a poor demented soul," said Rosaline. "Let me get you some cocoa."

"All right," said Francis and went to ring up Orange. But there was no news.

"Have a nice cup of fresh coffee," said la Marie, "and I'll tell you your cards. You'll marry a dark lady and come into money. You also have a bit of trouble coming to you."

"I'm not surprised," said Francis. "Will he come back?"

"I should say not," said la Marie.

That night some workmen from Montpellier sang songs in the café and shook their heads over Francis's story as told by Rosaline. "We don't think he'll come back," they said. All next day Francis telephoned Orange, but still there was no news. He went for a swim in the river, which was icy and brown with rains from the mountains. "He's probably committing suicide," said Rosaline. "And his poor little corpse will be washed into the sea with all that dead wood. Ah! his poor mother."

Amelia telephoned and said her father felt too tired to come today, would Rosaline send the luggage? Rosaline said no, she would not. When Francis was told, he sat on the terrace cursing and blaspheming loudly. Rosaline said he shouldn't say such awful things. All of a sudden he fell silent with his mouth hanging open—Uncle Ubriaco was riding into the square on Darling Little Mabel, his coat torn and face bleeding. He looked as if he'd spent an hour or more with a pair of mad tigers. Francis could only stare and stare as he mounted the steps.

Uncle Ubriaco took his hand and started explaining something about an awful time. Francis couldn't say how long it was since they'd entered the café when Rosaline popped in with a ghastly face.

"She's coming," she said rapidly and bolted the door. Sure enough, a second later there were thumping and screaming outside. Francis went out and Amelia slapped his face.

"This looks definitive," Francis said to Ubriaco. "Are you going to send her away or are you going away?" Ubriaco shook his head, looking miserable.

"I don't know," he replied.

"You must know," said Francis. "Which would you rather do?"

"I don't know," said Ubriaco again, darting furtive looks from one to the other. Amelia was giggling.

"Then for Hell's sake, go," said Francis. Rosaline went to collect the luggage.

"And go quickly," continued Francis. "I can't stand this. I want to be left alone." He averted his eyes from the two bicycles. Ten minutes later they were gone.

Amelia was riding Roger of Kildare and put out her tongue at Francis as they left.

Francis stood bleakly on the terrace. All the village were leaning out their windows, enthralled with the distraction. Without looking at anything, Francis directed his steps to the church, stood in the middle of the aisle, opened his trousers, and urinated.

In the steps of my good Saviour,
Like all us good believers,
I open up my trousers,
And bless with holy water.

Then he bowed to the altar with his trousers still open and departed. He went down to the river, which was swollen with a hemorrhage of mud and dead wood. The site of the tent was invisible. Francis thought he saw two ghosts through the water: Ubriaco and himself. He stripped off his jacket and shirt and started swimming across towards Mâze. The current was strong but he managed at last to reach the other side, breathless.

Then he climbed the hill to Mâze. He noted that the country was tarnished with the first yellows of autumn and felt suddenly glad that summer was gone. Once more he found himself in the streets of Mâze, which seemed darker and more abandoned than before. Trailing vines dropped across his face as he passed, and once a bird dropped in his path and spattered the white dust with blood as it hit the ground. The crickets trilled ferociously, till he had the illusion that his skull was filled with them and each was trying to outshrill the other. The noise gave him a pain behind his eyes.

Brambles appeared to have sprung up in the chapel garden and clawed each other with long, bristling arms. The smell of miraldalocks was as heavy as incense.

Francis plucked himself a bunch and sat down at the foot of the rocks in the chapel.

He decided to eat the plants. The prickly little leaves tickled the inside of his mouth, and the taste was strong and rank. He felt like a cow chewing the cud—it was difficult and unpleasant to swallow. A bird hopped in through the unpaved window and in a contralto that went vibrating through the chapel, sang as if this was its last song. The bird was a magpie. A flight of small bats took up the chorus; they were singing Bach's Mass in B Minor.

Miraldalocks herself sang the *Et in Unum* with the magpie: the hysterical notes went almost too high for ears to hear, and Francis thought the chapel walls must split. It was an admirable performance. They were all foaming at the mouth at the end. The bats were so moved that they whirled around higher and higher, long after the mass was ended. Miraldalocks washed her face and dipped her feet in blue water. A long table was carried in and covered with linen. Flunkeys carrying fruits, wine, and other foods laid the table; a banquet began. Francis sat at the foot of the table and watched rose trees grow out of the white linen tablecloth up to the ceiling, make a complicated design, and slide back down the walls. Blossoms of all colors opened out; black, red, white, blue, and purple, all with variations.

"You'll feel better soon," shouted Miraldalocks from the other end of the table. "You must pull yourself together." The room was filling with a torrent of water that had already reached the edges of the table. Francis saw Miraldalocks beckon to a flunkey and whisper in his ear; then she pointed in Francis's direction. The flunkey disappeared and was soon at his side with a huge rattle on a silver salver. Francis decided there was only one thing to do with a rattle, so he shook it. The noise was between a boom and a deafening crackle; he found this very pleasant. Miraldalocks clapped her hands and shouted "Tantivy!" The flunkeys waded about serving the victuals waist deep in water. Francis saw himself reflected and was surprised to find his head had grown and changed into that of a horse, though apparently his body had not altered. "Do you like it?" yelled Miraldalocks. "I think it suits you!"

"Yes," said Francis. "But how long is it going to last?"

"Oh you'll always be like that now," she replied, gaily. "I know somebody who's had a pig's head from birth!"

All the guests had begun pulling crackers and were showing each other their gifts. There were poisonous snakes, nightingales, strings of artificial pearls so long they had no end, live rabbits, revolvers, bowie knives, and red-hot pennies. Soon the table was covered. A little girl dressed as a Christmas angel was standing on the table reciting an astonishingly obscene poem; everybody yelled with glee and pinched her legs, stuck pins in her bottom, and fired bullets at her head. She remained aloof and went on with her poem in a schoolroom singsong. When she'd finished, Miraldalocks drowned her by holding her head underwater till the bubbles stopped coming up. Her bedraggled corpse began to float around the table, and people threw things at it languidly.

"This banquet is in your honour, you know," announced Miraldalocks. "I think you ought to give us a speech, Francis!"

Francis climbed onto the table obediently, bowed, touched his heart, and sat down again amidst rousing cheers.

The next entertainment was a staged fight between a buck rabbit and a fighting cock on a space cleared in the middle of the table. The rabbit defended himself heroically till he got both his eyes pecked out; then it got more difficult. Death came quite soon, with the rabbit screaming his end amongst his own offal. The cock hopped on top of the body and crowed.

Miraldalocks snatched it by one long spurred leg and tied it into her hair by the feet. It struggled and flapped to get free, making a wonderful headdress of darting greens and gold above Miraldalocks's hideous countenance. In the next interval a delicately carved minstrels' gallery grew out of the rock wall, filled with a female choir and two male harpers, all dressed simply, as ancient Greeks. They played the whole of Handel's *Messiah*. A gold cage was set on the table. It contained a chattering monkey trying to get out. Here the guests joined in the fun by making the most twisted grimaces at the raging monkey. Then, when it appeared to be furious enough to be tearing at its own flesh, somebody opened the cage and it flew straight at Francis amidst shouts of laughter. Francis dug at the clawing, hairy body and tried to shake it off. At last he drew his penknife and stabbed several times till the monkey dropped, inert and bleeding, into the water. Everybody roared with amusement, and the harpers struck up a Victorian march. Francis waved his rattle and neighed, not wanting to appear to be out of the spirit of the thing.

The cabaret ended with a grand finale of locusts and a vampire bat, who carried on a ferocious battle in the air. Dead locusts dropped onto the table and into the plates like hail. The snapping of the flying bat sounded like a machine gun above the sizzling of the locusts' wings. The bat slaughtered nearly every locust apart from a few halfhearted stragglers, and came to rest on Miraldalocks's bare forearm, taking refreshment from her blood. She clipped him onto her wrist like a falcon, much to the fury of the cock dancing about on her head.

"We'll let them kill each other later," she said, rising to her feet and reciting Baudelaire:

Il faut être toujours ivre. Tout est là: C'est l'unique question. Pour ne pas sentir l'horrible fardeau du

Temps qui brise vos épaules et vous penche vers la terre, il faut vous enivrer sans trêve.

Mais de quoi? De vin, de poésie ou de Vertu, à votre guise.

Mais enivrez-vous!

Il est l'heure de s'enivrer!

Pour n'être pas les esclaves martyrisés du temps, enivrez-vous; enivrez-vous sans cesse! De vin, de poésie ou de vertu, à votre guise.

One should always be drunk. That's the great thing; the only question. Not to feel the horrible burden of Time weighing on your shoulders and bowing you to the earth, you should be drunk without respite.

Drunk with what? With wine, with poetry, or with virtue, as you please. But get drunk.

"It is Time to get drunk! If you are not to be the martyred slaves of Time, be perpetually drunk! With wine, with poetry, or with virtue, as you please."

Francis found himself weeping and clapping with enthusiasm. He then also rose to his feet and replied with more Baudelaire:

Tu sais bien, Ô Satan,
Patron de ma détresse,
Que je n'allais pas là pour répandre un vain pleur;
Mais comme un vieux paillard d'une vieille maîtresse,
Je voulais m'enivrer de l'énorme catin
Dont le charme infernal me rajeunit sans cesse.

Que tu dormes encore dans les draps du matin,
Lourde, obscure, enrhumée, ou que tu te pavanes
Dans les voiles du soir passementés d'or fin,

Je t'aime, Ô capitale infâme! Courtisanes

Et bandits, tels souvent vous offrez des plaisirs
Que ne comprennent pas les vulgaires profanes.

But you, O Satan, patron of my pain,
Know I went not to weep for them in vain.

But like old lecher to old mistress goes,
Seeking but rapture, I sought out this trull
Immense, whose hellish charm resuscitates.

Whether in morning sheets you lie asleep,
Hidden and heavy with a cold, or flaunt
Through night in golden spangled veils,

Infamous City, I adore you! Courtesans
And bandits, you offer me such joys,
The common herd can never understand.

"I am your patron saint," screamed Miraldalocks, and they began to file out of the chapel through the seething water. The harps played the *Nachtmusik*, and the choir sang out "The Lost Chord" to the same tune. A carriage was waiting outside, and Francis got in with Miraldalocks. "Drive quickly," she shouted to the coachman, "and don't scrape the coat of arms on the gatepost going in."

They set off at a rumbling gallop, and night flew past the windows. Every now and again the carriage would give a lurch as if they'd run over something. Francis felt drunk and slightly sick. He couldn't remember having eaten anything at his banquet, though he knew there'd been great quantities of food. They stopped so suddenly that the horses slid several yards on their rumps. They were in a large courtyard filled with excited people. In the center of the crowd some workmen were erecting a guillotine on a raised platform. The proceedings were lighted with arc lamps.

"Hooray, we're on time," cried Miraldalocks, rubbing her hands. The cock crowed on her head. "I've reserved the royal box," she told Francis. "We ought to get a wonderful view."

They were ushered into their red plush seats by a lackey. Miraldalocks leaned over to criticise the crowd beneath them.

"But what are we going to see?" asked Francis. "You've told me nothing."

Miraldalocks chuckled with secret delight.

"That's a surprise," she said, poking him painfully in the ribs with a sharp forefinger. "Just wait and see."

A brass band had assembled at the far end of the platform and struck up the national anthem. Each player wore a blue ribbon stretched across his stomach. The executioner, a small man wearing a bowler hat, carried on a large wicker basket with a lid, which he placed scrupulously on the other side of the guillotine. He removed the lid and bowed to the crowd: the basket was filled with lilies. A murmur went up. Next came the priest. He did not raise his head but kept reading prayers aloud from a book in his hands. He stood to attention on the right side of the guillotine. Two servants sprinkled the area around the guillotine with rice powder. The crowd fell silent in expectation. The space to the left of the guillotine was taken up by a huge wooden horse decorated with ribbons and flowers, lifted onto the platform by a pulley.

"Do you want a box of chocolates or an orange?" whispered Miraldalocks. "The man's coming around. You can get them free this evening."

"No," said Francis. "I don't want anything, thank you." The night was lit all at once with rockets that went crackling in a menacing fashion towards the new moon. In the sudden bright light a door swung open on the left of the courtyard, and the crowd made a wavering gangway to admit three darkly clad individuals. As they mounted the platform, Francis saw that the smallest of the three bore a striking resemblance to himself before he'd grown a horse's head. His hands were tied and he wore pale grey tights and a black jerkin. He knew then he was to be executed. "I can't stay and watch this," Francis told Miraldalocks. "It really can't be done."

"Shhh," said Miraldalocks, absorbed in the spectacle. "What will people say if you chatter all the time?" Francis stayed in his place.

"Have you anything to say?" boomed the executioner to the boy. "Or any last request?" There was no reply. The priest offered him a tin of bull's eyes, which he produced out of his cassock. "These will help take your mind off it," he said. Still the boy made no move.

"Come along little chap," said one of the warders, taking a glimpse at his watch. "We can't stand here all night." He led the boy gently to the guillotine and put a cushion under his knees. The boy said, "Thank you." They were the only words he spoke.

The priest started gibbering prayers as if making up for lost time, as the executioner pulled a handle and the guillotine snapped off the boy's head, which leapt neatly into the basket of lilies, spurting a little jet of blood on the executioner's new trousers. A groan went up from the crowd, quickly followed by loud, unanimous cheers, in which Miraldalocks joined heartily. Francis noticed a little black ram and a little white ram jump out of the basket, circle the guillotine twice, and leap into the crowd.

"Take a good look at the platform," said Miraldalocks. "Isn't it rather lovely? We're going to meet the architect tonight at my reception! He's a real genius, and a Russian as well. He has the most delicious wit."

They waited for the crowd to disperse before they left their seats. "I tried to get the executioner to come," she explained. "It would have been thrilling to meet him! However, he sent his very deepest regrets and said he was obliged to attend a military banquet. However," she said, "there is one man coming who once cleaned out the condemned cell: so we shall have quite a few celebrities!"

They drove to Miraldalocks's château, where hundreds of flunkeys were preparing a cold buffet in the antechamber. Persian vases filled with liquors lined the brocaded walls; piles of ham sandwiches, turkeys, pastries, and boxes of sardines took up every inch of the thirty-foot table. In the center of the apartment was a monstrous glass bowl of punch containing live trout that swam drunkenly to and fro.

"I thought the trout rather original," said Miraldalocks, "without being too showy. Artistic people like wandering around, you know, and just helping themselves! I like free and easy hospitality. Don't you?"

The guests were beginning to arrive, and a majordomo announced them at the top of a wide staircase that descended into the antechamber. This gave Miraldalocks a good opportunity of scanning each one as they descended. The warmth of her reception varied according to the importance of the individual guest. Some were in evening dress and others amazingly filthy, with beards, and carrying portfolios or sketchbooks. They wore an abstracted air and anything they said was rude.

"It's really aesthetic candor," whispered Miraldalocks. "They haven't time to bandy polite twaddle; they are occupied with higher things."

Their women wore rags and strange knitted caps and sandals; they talked loudly and assertively about higher subjects.

The punch bowl was entirely hidden by guests who used any means, fair or foul, to obtain the biggest drink. Nobody took the slightest notice of either Miraldalocks or Francis. They could not get near the buffet, where the food was being torn to pieces and either eaten or flung on the floor. Those who were too weak to carve a place at the table stood in groups talking. Francis kept hearing the words *Significant form* and *Plastic expression*. Nobody laughed. "Don't dare mention any kind of game except darts," added Miraldalocks. She was watching the guests carefully with a worried frown.

"Nobody seems surprised at my horse's head," remarked Francis. "I'd have thought it's rather out of the ordinary."

"My dear! Don't you know it's horribly bourgeois to be surprised at anything?"

Miraldalocks was craning her neck; suddenly her brow cleared. The Majordomo waved a white handkerchief discreetly. "That's the signal," she said with repressed excitement.

"He's coming!"

"Egres Lepereff!" boomed the Majordomo, raising his voice several semitones. The great architect paused on the top steps so that everybody could get a good look. He was dressed as a Cossack. He carried his head between his shoulders in such a way as to intensify the immense length of his curved though elegant nose. He descended the stairs gracefully, twitching his nostrils like a racehorse.

Miraldalocks was off in a second, racing to engage him in conversation before anybody else. Francis, terrified to be left alone, raced after her. The Great Architect scarcely replied to her greeting and drew a blueprint out of his pocket, which he scanned indifferently before replying to her.

"But what a wonderful feat of machinery, your platform!" she was saying. "I hardly noticed what was going on, my senses were so delighted with the Form!"

"Good machinery and efficient planning," said Egres Lepereff, "are always aesthetically moving. My platform," he continued, looking in the other direction, "was pleasing, though utterly devoid of anything save the merest mechanical necessities. It was a symphony of pure form."

"What a monster brain," Miraldalocks whispered in Francis's ear.

"Architecture," continued the great man, "in modern art is the nearest form to pure abstraction."

Francis felt obliged to say something intelligent so he tried. "But if you build abstract houses, the more abstract you make them the less there'll be there, and if you get abstraction itself there won't be anything at all."

"It takes a certain time to grasp; these things are not included in elementary education," replied Egres Lepereff, taking a sniff through the whole length of his nose.

"What wit!" whispered Miraldalocks.

"An intellectual aristocracy," he continued, "on a purely abstract basis with a smattering of Marx's social system, is the only way I can find of rendering the world less uninhabitable for intelligent human beings."

"Did you enjoy the execution?" said Francis, with another effort at conversation.

"I wasn't there," he replied, raising his eyebrows slightly. "I do not believe in capital punishment nor in mingling in the entertainments of the poor. I hold that individual milieus should stay in their own circles and refrain from sightseeing amongst their less fortunate neighbours."

"But I thought you weren't class conscious," said Francis.

"This," replied Egres distantly, "can only be settled on the abstract basis. Mere vulgar curiosity should be controlled." He cast Francis a look of loathing and sipped a glass of cold water.

"What is your opinion of the intellectual side of the execution?" asked Miraldalocks, bending forward eagerly to catch every word of the reply.

"Merely paradoxical," he replied. "The defendant was but a common little guttersnipe, only good for the streets and a rapid burial in quicklime. One of the many depressing hangers-on to that dreary old bicycle king. All those people make me tired." He yawned languidly and drew out a sad-looking newspaper with a title in black print like the letters on a mortuary card: THE SPEW MATESMAN. WEEKLY REVIEW FOR PROGRESSIVE INTELLECTUALS. By this time nearly all the guests were dead drunk and either strewn about the floor or propped up against the walls. Miraldalocks was also pretty well incoherent and soon sank to the floor unconscious. Francis slipped away unobserved and composed himself to sleep in an alcove near the now deserted buffet.

Egres Lepereff continued to probe his journal near the center of the chamber, the only upright member of the community. After five minutes he looked up and gave a frown; then his gaze fell on the buffet, and a great change came over him as he fixed a luminous eye on a large jar of gherkins and pickled onions. For a second or two he stared at the jar, then, making sure he was not observed, tiptoed towards it, saliva drooling. He fell on the jar with the most astonishing gluttony Francis had ever seen, stuffing the pickles into his mouth so that streams of vinegar ran down his chin and onto his beautiful silk shirt. He did not pause till the enormous jar was empty. He then repaired the damage of his strange meal.

Francis stepped out of his alcove. With the look of a snake at bay, Egres Lepereff picked up a carving knife and just missed pinning Francis to the wall; then he whirled, snarling horribly, and quit the room, rapidly negotiating the long flight of the stairs.

Francis thought he might as well take a drink, so he helped himself to a bottle of beer, which he was obliged to drink out of a soup plate owing to the equine construction of his mouth. He noticed that above each of the sleeping figures hung a meager ghost, rather like a piece of string that had been starved to death. Francis surmised they were their own respective ghosts, or spectres of a thin variety (ghosts are usually of a fattish nature, though there are exceptions). Francis thought it would be rather amusing to knot them together; it took him some time to tie the whole lot together with a bow at each join. They offered no resistance save a gentle swaying, as if a light breeze were passing through the antechamber. The guests snored on oblivious. A small buff hen came hopping down the stairs making a great clucking. She paused, laid an egg that split immediately on the hard parquet floor, and then addressed the cock who was reposing wearily on Miraldalocks's head. He stirred, tried to rise, and sank back into a deep sleep. The hen became hysterical and furious, and Francis had to free the cock to stop the noise. Then they both retired, grumbling.

Francis searched the château for an exit. There were long deserted corridors lined with decadent sculpture and abstract oil paintings, copies of Greek gods, and family photographs. At length he found the kitchen, where the servants' breakfast was already cooking. Here he received instructions for his return to Saint-Roc.

The sun was already sinking when Francis reached the river. He had met nobody during his journey. Indeed the country he passed through seemed to have been swept by plague, it was so deserted. Rosaline gave a cry when he entered the café: "We thought you were dead and gone!" she exclaimed. "The undertaker has already dug your grave near those cypress trees you liked so much. He said he might as well get it done while business is slack."

"Well, I'm sorry," said Francis, noticing one or two clients staring at him curiously over their Pernods and whispering.

"You look peculiar," said Rosaline. "I would hardly have known you."

"I've not slept for two nights," said Francis.

Rosaline held a whispered consultation with the

Pernod drinkers. "It's probably sorrow that's done it," she was saying. "I've heard of things like that happening before. Come here," she said aloud. "Come into the kitchen." She took a mirror off the wall, and Francis gazed at his horse's face. "Good gracious!" he said. "And I had clean forgotten!"

Rosaline's trade boomed. People poured in from far and wide to see the boy with the horse's head brought about by a broken heart. Rosaline deducted five francs from the price of Francis's room. "After all, it's you who're filling the *caisse*," she explained. On Sundays and even weekdays there was enormous competition to feed Francis drinks and hear him talk.

"Ask for champagne when they look prosperous," she told Francis. But Rosaline's champagne was like immensely sweet soda water, and Francis really preferred beer. Still, Rosaline cursed him so much he was obliged to comply, and many a night went to bed sick. "You drink too much," Rosaline told him once. And in would come a prosperous customer and Francis would be obliged once more to swell his stomach to the bursting point.

He gave up washing and stayed alone as much as he could, which wasn't much. All through the day he kept being called into the café to show himself to the gentlemen. At first he rather enjoyed the notoriety, but after a few weeks he longed for peace and would take long solitary walks in the evenings, when his head was less noticeable. He usually went past the seven cypress trees in the cemetery, since this road was the least haunted. Sometimes he would stand for long periods shouting across at Mâze and hearing his voice echo back, hollow and changed but still his own voice.

Uncle Ubriaco wrote often, asking him to come to Paris, and sent him books, few of which Francis was allowed the opportunity to read. He kept the letters and knew them all by heart. He now took his meals in the kitchen with Rosaline and her mother and had suddenly got a great repugnance for meat and would watch the old woman drink her mixture of blood and milk with a turning stomach. He lived on tinned peas, garlic, and pumpkin soup. Simon comforted him with his moist eyes when Rosaline shouted fit to crack his eardrums. But Francis could not go away; roots seemed to have sprung out of the soles of his feet into the earth of Saint-Roc. He had no active desire to go away. The country was hysterical with color and the snails plentiful. But Francis had vowed never to eat a snail again. The harvest had begun and the entire village was dyed purple with crushed grapes. Peasants were making their eau-de-vie, and the steam scented the streets and houses. Lorries with tanks of marc were seen to come and go with a shattering noise. The strength and degree of each individual eau-de-vie was discussed, chez la Marie, chez Rosaline, and in the square near the statue of Saint-Roc.

Simon kept Francis supplied with liquor now that his fig tree yielded no more. The aubergines too were nearly over. Francis did his own washing at the river amongst the village women. He told them gossip and tailored those that lacked colour with his imagination. The water was cold and dark, but the conversation rolled along pleasantly enough. The more respectable people of the village shunned Francis, but in general his popularity reigned supreme. Rosaline was tender or ferocious according to how much Francis pampered her. One day he bought a pair of *sabots* and purple socks in Pontfantôme and hobbled around the village proudly. He received a few wounds from stones flung by the children, but otherwise nobody took much notice. Noël once gave him a ride in his *charrette* drawn by a mule, causing general excitement and laughter. Rosaline approved it as a publicity stunt and had the inspiration to borrow the gramophone from Pontfantôme that they'd used for the Cafard hindou. The gramophone owner complied, on condition that Francis come fetch it himself and appear on display at three different cafés. So they got the gramophone and Francis was obliged to do polkas, paso dobles, and javas all Sunday afternoon; some people were bold enough to dance with him.

One day the local dentist asked him to go to Marseilles for the weekend. "Only," he warned, "don't tell anybody. My family would be displeased to know I associate with you." Francis promised, as he thought it might be nice to get a change of air for two days. The doctor said a taxi would call for Francis after dark and they would meet on the bridge of Pontfantôme, where he would be waiting in his own motorcar.

"He's very chic and rich," said Rosaline, "so I think you may be permitted to go."

So Francis went to Marseilles. They partook of a huge dinner and afterwards the doctor said he wanted Francis to meet a clever and distinguished friend. Francis felt drunk enough to meet anybody. So they drove to a tall house in a back street. The door was opened by a grumbling Oriental and they were ushered into a heavily scented apartment where, in a corner, stood a large cage, just about Francis's fit. He took a quick look at the cage and was out of the room and down the stairs, galloping for his life. He seemed to run a long way through devious alleys before he stopped to breathe. A shadow that passed on the opposite wall bore a strange resemblance to Uncle Ubriaco on Darling Little Mabel.

"Ubriaco! Ubriaco!" screamed Francis, beginning to run after the retreating bicycle. "Wait for me, Uncle Ubriaco! I'm coming! It's me, Francis!" He felt the tears welling out of his big horse's eyes. The bicycle stopped and as Francis ran up panting, crying, and laughing, he was faced by a total stranger. "Get away you monster," said the man, terrified, and started shouting for policemen. Two came running up; Francis spent the night in prison for assault and battery.

In the evening he arrived at Saint-Roc in a depressed

frame of mind and gave Rosaline an account of his adventures. "Tell nobody else," she warned. "The doctor's a respected and rich gentleman. He has bought nearly a dozen champagnes within the last month!"

Francis wrote at length to Uncle Ubriaco.

Rosaline received several offers of money for Francis but she always refused. "I am very attached to him," she explained, "though I often scold him."

Francis began to love the nights and he always went to bed as early as he was allowed. Once lying down, he would go promenading through dreams till morning. One night he dreamt he was a black wolf in a forest. He came upon a round castle with windows at ground level, which he peeped through fearfully. He saw a huge fancy-dress ball: Pfoebe was there, featured in black velvet tights and a toothbrush moustache. "It's not what I want," he said to himself, going a little further on and creeping into the castle through a hole that scarcely admitted him. He was in a narrow passageway terminating in a revolving door at the other side of which was a twelve-foot drop into a medieval street. A little white dog was barking up at him. I must get down and kill it, thought Francis, but he couldn't get through the revolving door.

Sometimes he wrote poems, all of which he dedicated to himself.

> *I think I am an oyster, walking down the street*
> *Walking down the street, though I haven't any feet:*
> *Roses roses, all around my door—*
> *Offal! Offal! Haberdash. Dictionaries! Saws.*

He wrote a ballad too, "The Ascension of Iscariot," which was much better.

> *Iscariot he built a ship,*
> *And if I'm told aright,*

He did not build it in the day
Nor even in the night.

He built it in the dusk,
And he built it in the dawn,
He worked extremely hard,
Till his hands and nails were torn.

It might have been a ship,
And it might have been a house.
The bridge was like a kidney shape,
The figurehead a louse.

The ship was drawn by pigs,
And they said they said they said
That it smelt as if Iscariot,
Iscariot was dead.

"You're right," said he, Iscariot.
"Since twenty moons have passed
"I made my will and said my prayers
"And breathed up my last.

"My will and my last testament
"I wrote and signed each one.
"I sealed & stamped & stamped & sealed
"And now my day is done.

"I'm ascending into Heaven
"In the ship you've seen me make.
"Amen! Amen! Amen! May Peter
"Open up the gates."

The next was entitled "Loss of Caste." (There has been remarkable controversy regarding the meter of this poem.)

They constructed a dilemma—
The Council board provided
   steel, screws, rocks, and plans.
I walked beneath to look, I was interested.
It crumbled and fell at my vibrating steps.

*I am now flat.
I cannot wear my hat. My hat oh God
  my hat.
Why? because my head is flat.*

There was also one poem in French, written on a piece of cardboard, the left cover of which was stained with grape juice:

*Ne fais pas cela mon ami.
Ne me regarde pas comme ça
À travers l'eau qui coule en remuant
Ma vision de tes
Deux yeux bleus
Comme des poissons bleus toujours attachés
Comme deux lunes bleues
Comme deux ailes bleues très bleues
Comme deux jumeaux bleus
qui ne se sont jamais vus entre eux
Mais restent collés éternellement
les deux frères bleus.
S'il vous plaît ne me regardez plus.*

The café had four habitual clients who arrived each evening, drank a coffee and some of their own marc, played two turns of Russian billiards, and afterwards told stories. They always sat at the middle table with Francis and Rosaline, who stayed with them unless a richer client should happen to come in, whereupon Francis would be called upon to entertain.

Thursday evening usually drew a blank as far as champagne went, so the old clients stayed later and talked more freely. "I knew a bullfighter in Nîmes," said the first veteran, "who was the strangest man I ever knew. He had a face like a big toe and treated the bulls like rats. Jorge González the Savage they called him, and few people knew why, for out of the bullring he seemed a quiet, sentimental man. My friend Joseph knew González's family well and tells several anecdotes about Don Jorge. Perhaps you remember? The scandal concerned a certain English lady of quality by the name of The Honourable Mrs. Bigge. A middle-aged widow of means, but not even the most biased observer could have called the lady attractive. Joseph was taking an aperitif with the bullfighter in one of the larger cafés. And Mrs. Bigge was at the next table, alone. 'There's a rich foreigner,' said González. 'I could do nicely with a wife like that. I could retire and have a villa in Monte Carlo. It is a pity such women all seem to be so ugly. Look at her nose.' And he became very moody. In the meantime the English lady had recognized González and addressed him in bad French. 'Oh Mr. González, I saw you fighting those awful bulls yesterday and I was simply thrilled.' González immediately invited her to their table and talked and talked about his different feats. From that day González and Mrs. Bigge were seen together every day. Then one evening González invited her to his room for coffee after dinner. He filled her up with *kummel* till she lost her reserve and proposed: this was exactly what González intended. 'Certainly,' he replied, and then by some unknown means persuaded Mrs. Bigge to let him make a 'little operation' on her nose. 'After which,' he assured her, 'he would be madly in love.'

"On one of his various travels González had learnt the art of tattooing, and now he decorated Mrs. Bigge's nose with flowers, fruits, and birds, all very neatly executed from the bridge to the tip and around the nostrils. Apparently the pain of this procedure sobered her up, but the bullfighter held her securely till he was quite finished; that is, till he had crowned his handiwork by piercing her nose with a red-hot needle and inserting a ring. I believe the screams were terrific, even after he stuffed her mouth with her own stocking. This is how Mrs. Bigge was found, tied to the bedpost by a string attached at the other end to the ring in her nose.

"Of course she made a great case against González and with all her influence and money not only got him put in prison but ruined him financially. Jorge González was never a very rich man.

"A short time after he was put in prison Mrs. Bigge committed suicide; it was her last revenge on the bullfighter. Nothing more was heard of González, but I wouldn't be surprised to see him playing bulls once more in the Nîmes arena."

"I remember the scandal," said the second veteran. "But the newspapers never gave full details."

"Hushed up by the lady's family," explained the first. "It made González quite famous though, and he'd have done well out of the publicity had he not been in prison. Poor González! He always had a good head for business and I don't doubt he would have become a tolerably rich man if he had not that unfortunate perversion for noses."

Francis promised Rosaline the following morning that he would arise early and go hunting mushrooms. Rosaline had spied a big bucketful chez la Marie and was hot with jealousy. It was Sunday and the church bells were ringing. Descending to the kitchen, Francis found Rosaline was about and started to prepare his own coffee. Shortly she came in with a telegram for Francis. He opened it apprehensively and Rosaline read over his shoulder:

COME URGENTLY PARIS WITH ALL CLOTHES! UNCLE UBRIACO.

"I must go at once," said Francis. "I wonder what it means!"

"Perhaps it's not from him," said Rosaline darkly. "I would telephone first if I were you."

"He's not on the telephone," said Francis. "I must get to Orange tonight in time to catch the rapide."

The river swelled that day till it was over the square, past the statue of Saint-Roc, and up to the steps of the Café Pirigou. Amidst wailing and drinking in the café,

Francis embraced Rosaline and left in a boat rowed by Noël. A hired car awaited him on dry land, and by nightfall he was in Orange. On the train he was obliged to stand up all night in the noise and grime, while his fingers ticked on the suitcase without cease. The night, Francis thought, will never end.

They rushed and jolted through the darkness, hour after hour of nothing but sheets of black night. When the train reached the Gare de Lyon it was seven-thirty in the morning. Francis was surprised to see no one waiting for him on the platform, though he had replied to the wire immediately. He felt dreadfully weary and hungry, and people stared at him unpleasantly. He wondered how he would explain his horse's head to Uncle Ubriaco, but felt sure Ubriaco would understand.

He took a taxi right away to Uncle Ubriaco's. The tree outside gave no more shade but only flapped a few remaining yellow leaves. Francis pulled the creaking bell; Amelia opened the door. She stared at him openmouthed for a second and said, "Ah, you are a hideous monster, but I know who you are. Come in."

She led him into the workroom and locked the door on them. Francis noticed she was giggling, as if at some delightful joke.

"Where's Uncle Ubriaco?" demanded Francis peevishly. Amelia covered her mouth to stop her mirth.

"Gone." She gurgled. "Gone gone gone."

"What do you mean?" said Francis.

"He left yesterday to fetch you at Saint-Roc, and I thought it would be a good opportunity to get you here and tell your parents to come and fetch you out of our way."

Francis clouted Amelia once, twice, five times in all on each side of her head, with all his force, shouting, "Bitch bitch bitch." Amelia screamed and foamed and grabbed a hammer. Francis dodged in and out of semifabricated bicycles, avoiding his pursuer and the hammer. He tripped on a stray wheel, however, and was run to earth. Amelia whacked Francis in the head with the hammer till a big hole appeared in the horse's skull and streams of blood made a strangely shaped pool on the floor. Francis died almost immediately.

Suddenly frightened at what she'd done, Amelia ran into a corner and started whimpering. "I didn't mean to kill him Daddy, I only wanted to hurt him and I couldn't stop myself whacking and whacking till all the awful blood came bubbling and blackish—ugh!" She covered her face with her hands, shutting out what she felt to be an indecent spectacle. There was something private about the sprawling corpse and the bicycle wheel, making Amelia feel ashamed to look. She felt almost as if she was peeping in on somebody in the lavatory. A flight of pigeons rushed past the window, and a clock struck.

It was Hector who got Francis sealed in a plain deal coffin and sent off to England. It was Hector who wired Uncle Ubriaco at Saint-Roc and Hector who comforted Amelia, who could not forget how horrible Francis looked dead.

She tried long explanations to Uncle Ubriaco about how she hadn't really meant it, but he seemed to have grown dumb.

Uncle Ubriaco arrived at Crackwood the day after Francis. He entered a house of deep mourning. The hall was deserted; then a rushing of water and Francis's bereft mother stepped out of the lavatory. As soon as she saw Ubriaco she stopped dead, placed a hand on her heart, and stared at him dramatically. Then remembering her handkerchief, she covered her eyes and nose, apparently weeping, took a half turn, and supported herself on the table with one hand. She stood several seconds thus with bent head and averted face. Ubriaco wondered how long the dumb show would last. The house was in half darkness, each blind half pulled down over the windows; any of the servants who spoke spoke in whispers. The smell of lilies all over the house was death itself. Eventually the mother turned and beckoned Ubriaco to follow her. With a slow religious gesture she opened the door into the room of death. Francis's coffin was varnished white and surrounded by six monster candles and a veritable garden of lilies. Uncle Ubriaco stared angrily and said, "Oh Francis, Francis, they've put you in a white coffin! White! Red, yellow, even green—but surely not white."

The mother knelt at the foot of the coffin on a priedieu and started praying with her back to Uncle Ubriaco. A little dog nosed open the door, circled the coffin, lifted his leg gaily on the left corner, and went out again.

Ubriaco gave a slow smile.

The mother put in a few more prayers and rose to her feet slowly. The handkerchief came out appropriately, and they left the room.

Late that night Ubriaco crept down to the room of death carrying a brush and two pots of paint.

The candles had burnt lower and the odor of lilies was more overpowering than ever. Uncle Ubriaco thought sadly how much Francis had always loathed these flowers. He stood for a moment, contemplating the long white box, and then set to work. One of the pots of varnish was yellow, the other black. He made a gay waspish design with alternate stripes of yellow and black. The whole thing took some time but was neatly terminated before daylight. Uncle Ubriaco bowed profoundly to the striped coffin and left the house, mounted his push-bike, and pedalled away.

Thus ends the story of little Francis.

The childhood home of Leonora Carrington: Crookhey Hall, Cockerham, England. (Courtesy of Gabriel Weisz Carrington.)

Leonora Carrington as a young girl. (Courtesy of Gabriel Weisz Carrington.)

Miss Laura Carrington, one
last night's debutantes, in her
on the way to Buckingham Pal

ABOVE LEFT: Leonora Carrington, the young woman on a horse. (Courtesy of Gabriel Weisz Carrington.)

ABOVE RIGHT: Leonora's debut, misnomered. (Courtesy of Gabriel Weisz Carrington.)

OPPOSITE: Leonora Carrington and her mother on the day of her presentation at court. (Courtesy of Leonora Carrington.)

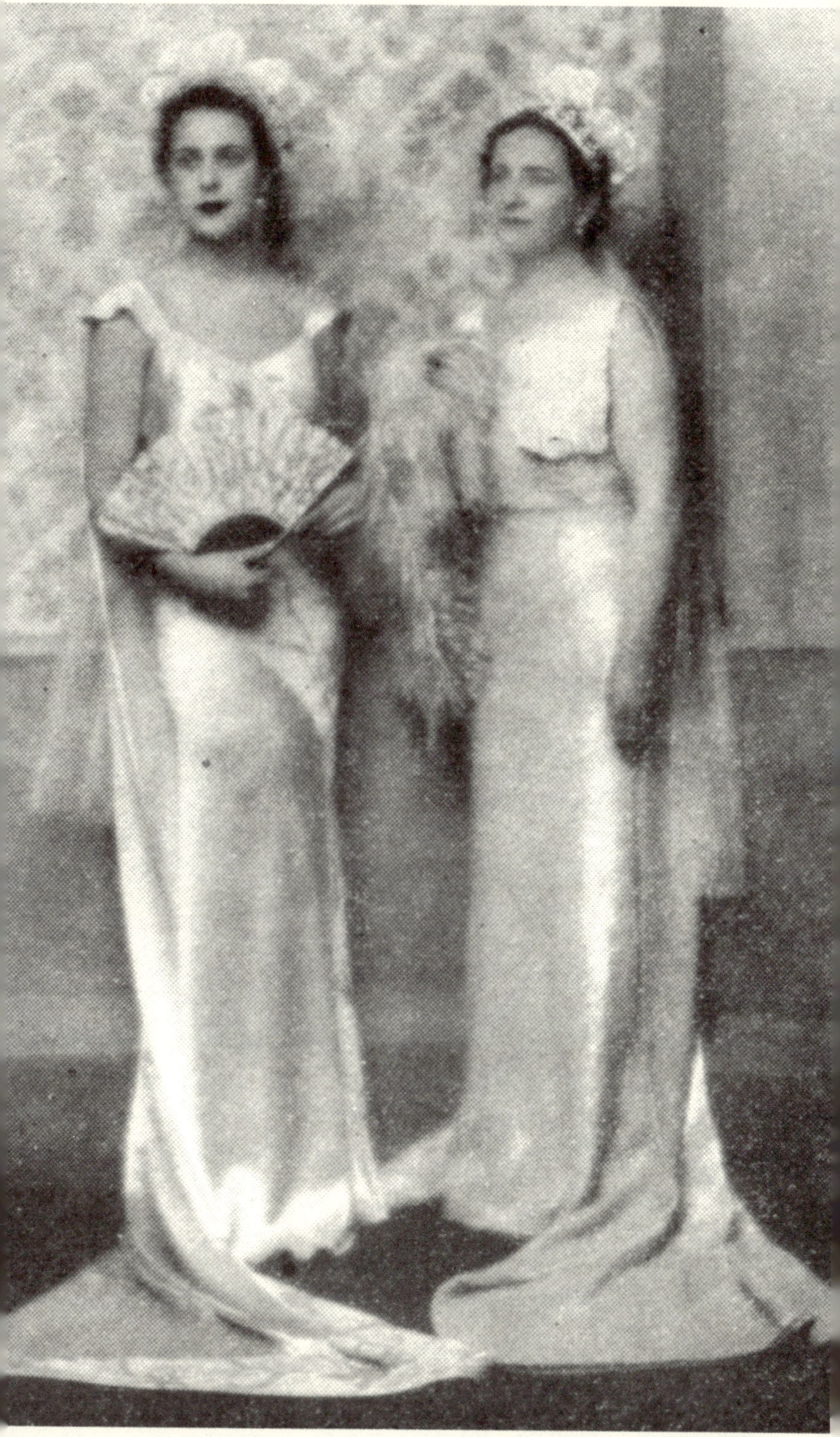

From left: E. L. T. Messens, Max Ernst, Leonora, and Paul Eluard, Paris, 1937. (Photograph copyright © Lee Miller Archives, 1985.)

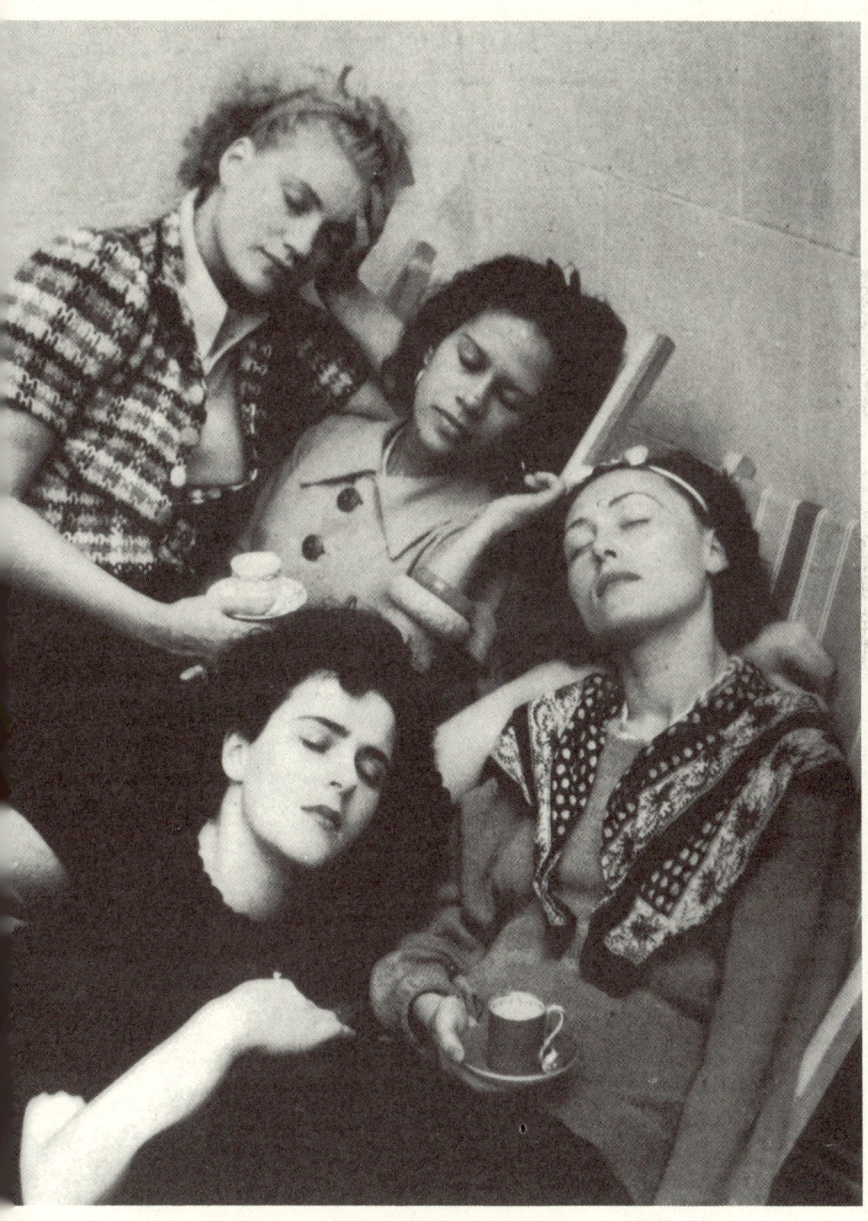

Leonora and friends at Lamb Creek, England, 1937. Clockwise from upper left: Lee Miller, Ady, Nusch Eluard, and Leonora. (Photograph copyright © Lee Miller Archives, 1985.)

ABOVE: *Max Ernst, the river and the village of Eguèze, 1938. (Courtesy Galerie 1900–2000, Paris.)*

BELOW: *Leonora Carrington, down by the river, 1938. (Courtesy Galerie 1900–2000, Paris.)*

*Leonora Carrington at Saint-Martin-d'Ardèche, 1939.
(Photograph copyright © Lee Miller Archives, 1985.)*

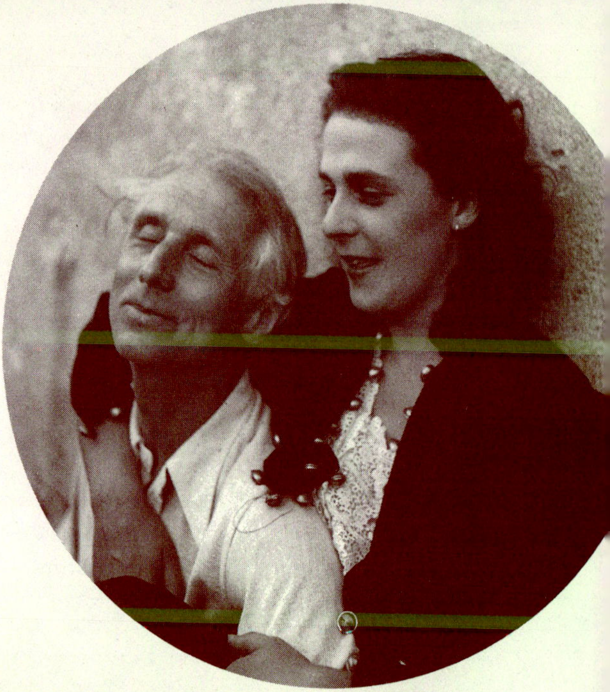

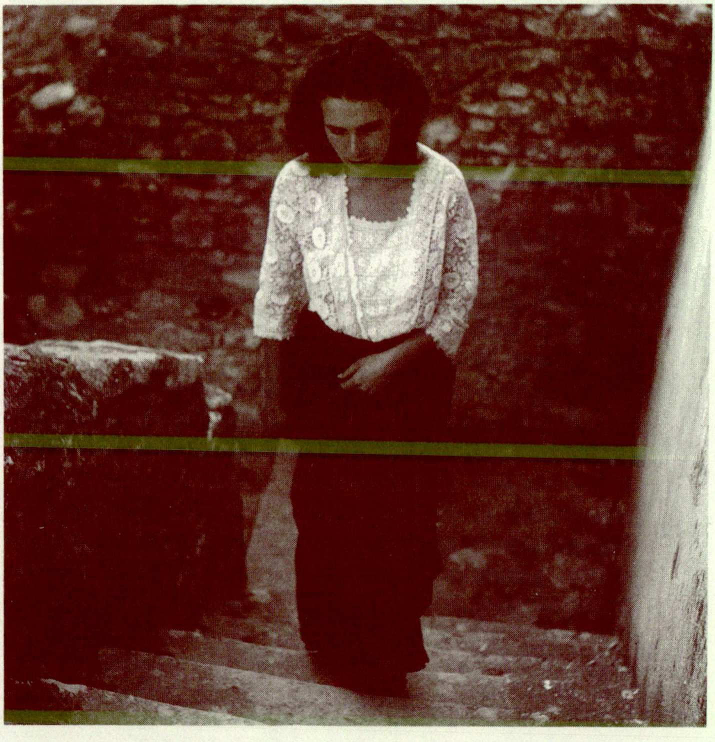

CLOCKWISE FROM BELOW: *Saint-Martin-d'Ardèche, 1939: The house; Leonora; Max and Leonora; Leonora. (All photographs copyright © Lee Miller archives, 1985.)*

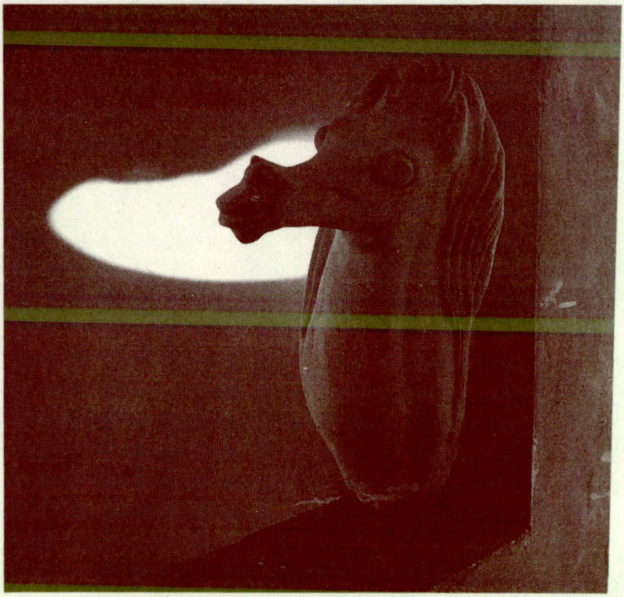
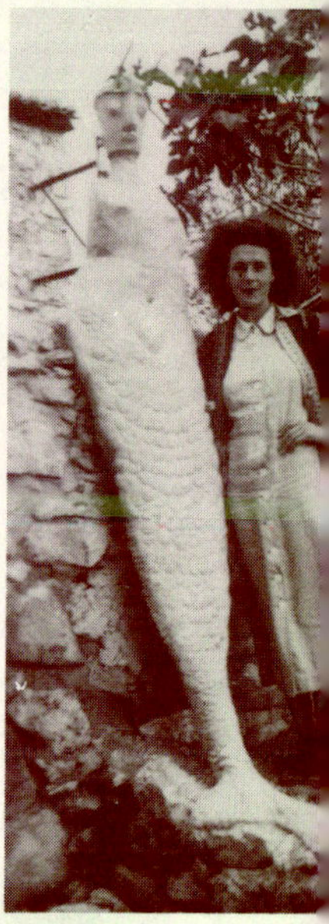
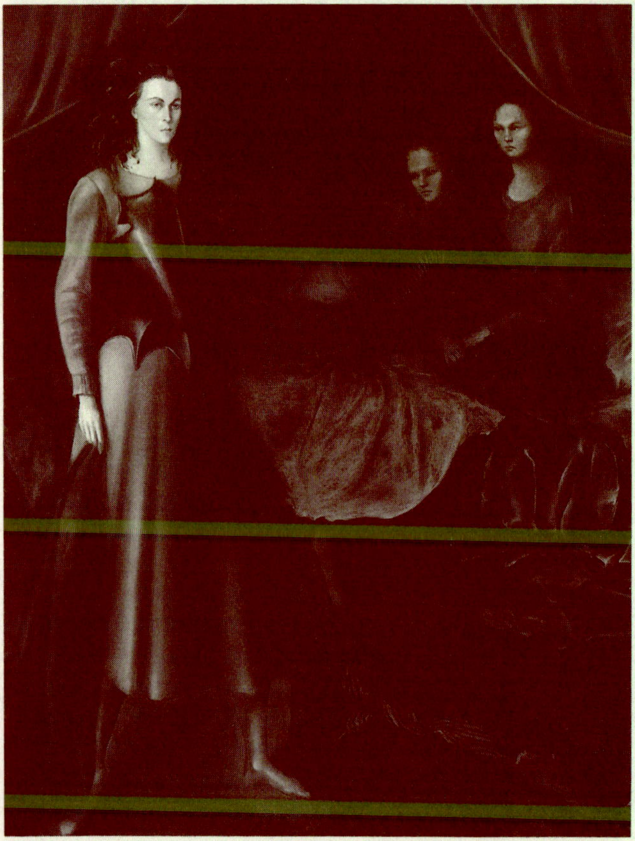

OPPOSITE ABOVE LEFT: Sculpture of a horse's head *by Leonora Carrington, Saint-Martin-d'Ardèche, 1939. (Photograph copyright © Lee Miller Archives, 1985.)*

OPPOSITE ABOVE RIGHT: Leonora with mermaid, *by Max Ernst, Saint-Martin-d'Ardèche, 1939. (Courtesy of Gabriel Weisz Carrington.)*

OPPOSITE: The Alcove: An Interior with Three Women, *by Leonor Fini, c. 1939. The main figure is Leonora Carrington. (Courtesy of The Edward James Foundation.)*

RIGHT: Portrait of Max Ernst, *by Leonora Carrington, c. 1939. (Courtesy of The Young-Mallin Collection.) Photograph by Laurent Sozzani.*

ABOVE: Double Portrait, the artist and Max Ernst, *by Leonora Carrington. Saint-Martin-d'Ardèche, 1940. (Courtesy of Dallas Ernst.)*

Artists in Exile, group photo Ernst-Guggenheim triplex, New York, 1942. Left to right, first row: Stanley William Hayter, Leonora Carrington, Frederick Kiesler, Kurt Seligmann; second row: Max Ernst, Amédée Ozenfant, André Breton, Fernand Léger, Berenice Abbott; third row: Jimmy Ernst, Peggy Guggenheim, John Ferren, Marcel Duchamp, Piet Mondrian. (Courtesy of Philadelphia Museum of Art, private collection.)

DOWN BELOW

Down Below

Monday, August 23, 1943

Exactly three years ago, I was interned in Dr. Morales's sanatorium in Santander, Spain, Dr. Pardo, of Madrid, and the British Consul having pronounced me incurably insane. Since I fortuituously met you, whom I consider the most clear-sighted of all, I began gathering a week ago the threads which might have led me across the initial border of Knowledge. I must live through that experience all over again, because, by doing so, I believe that I may be of use to you, just as I believe that you will be of help in my journey beyond that frontier by keeping me lucid and by enabling me to put on and to take off at will the mask which will be my shield against the hostility of Conformism.

Before taking up the actual facts of my experience, I want to say that the sentence passed on me by society at that particular time was probably, surely even, a godsend, for I was not aware of the importance of health, I mean of the absolute necessity of having a healthy body to avoid disaster in the liberation of the mind. More important yet, the necessity that others be with me that we may feed each other with our knowledge and thus constitute the Whole. I was not sufficiently conscious at the time of your philosophy to understand. *The time had not come for me to understand.* What I am going to endeavor to express here with the utmost fidelity was but an embryo of knowledge.

I begin therefore with the moment when Max was taken away to a concentration camp for the second time, under the escort of a gendarme who carried a rifle (May 1940). I was living in Saint-Martin-d'Ardèche. I wept for several hours, down in the village; then I went up again to my house where, for twenty-four hours, I indulged in voluntary vomitings induced by drinking orange blossom water and interrupted by a short nap. I hoped that my sorrow would be diminished by these spasms, which tore at my stomach like earthquakes. I know now that this was but one of the aspects of those vomitings: I had realised the injustice of society, I wanted first of all to cleanse myself, then go beyond its brutal ineptitude. My stomach was the seat of that society, but also the place in which I was united with all the elements of the earth. It was the *mirror* of the earth, the reflection of which is just as real as the person reflected. That mirror—my stomach—had to be rid of the thick layers of filth (the accepted formulas) in order properly, clearly, and faithfully to reflect the earth; and when I say "the earth," I mean of course all the earths, stars, suns in the sky and on the earth, as well as all the stars, suns, and earths of the microbes' solar system.

For three weeks I ate very sparingly, carefully eschewing meat, and drank wine and alcohol, feeding on potatoes and salad, at the rate perhaps of two potatoes a day. My impression is that I slept pretty well. I worked at my vines, astonishing the peasants by my strength. Saint John's Day was near at hand, the vines were beginning to blossom, they had to be sprayed often with sulphur. I also worked at my potatoes, and the more I sweated, the better I liked it, because this meant that I was getting purified. I took sunbaths, and my physical strength was such as I have never known before or afterwards.

Various events were taking place in the outside world: the collapse of Belgium, the entry of the Germans in France. All of this interested me very little and I had no fear whatsoever within me. The village was thronged with Belgians, and some soldiers who had entered my home accused me of being a spy and threatened to shoot me on the spot because someone had been looking for snails at night, with a lantern, near my house. Their threats impressed me very little indeed, for I knew that I was not destined to die.

After three solitary weeks, Catherine, an Englishwoman, a very old friend of mine, arrived, fleeing from Paris with Michel Lucas, a Hungarian. A week went by and I believe they noticed nothing abnormal in me. One day, however, Catherine, who had been for a long time under the care of psychoanalysts, persuaded me that my attitude betrayed an unconscious desire to get rid for the second time of my father: Max, whom I had to eliminate if I wanted to live. She begged me to cease punishing myself and to look for another lover. I think she was mistaken when she said I was torturing myself. I think that she interpreted me fragmentarily, which is worse than not to interpret at all. However, by doing so she restored me to sexual desire. I tried frantically to seduce two young men, but without success. They would have none of me. And I had to remain sadly chaste.

The Germans were approaching rapidly; Catherine frightened me and begged me to leave with her, saying that if I refused to do so, she too would remain. I accepted. I accepted above all because, in my evolution, Spain represented for me Discovery. I accepted because I expected to get a visa put in Max's passport in Madrid. I still felt bound to Max. This document, which bore his image, became an entity, as if I was taking Max with me. I accepted, somewhat touched by Catherine's arguments, which were distilling into me, hour after hour, a growing fear. For Catherine, the Germans meant rape. I was not afraid of that, I attached no importance to it. What caused panic to rise within me was the thought of robots, of thoughtless, fleshless beings.

Michel and I decided to go to Bourg-Saint-Andéol to secure a travelling permit. The gendarmes, totally indifferent and uninterested, kept on smoking cigarettes and refused to give us the bit of paper, barricading themselves behind phrases like "we can't do anything about it." We were unable to leave, yet I knew that we would leave the following day. We went to the notary, where I made over to the proprietor of the Motel des Touristes of Saint-Martin my house and all my goods. I returned home and spent the whole night carefully sorting the things I intended taking along with me. All of them got into a suitcase which bore, beneath my name, a small brass plate set into the leather, on which was written the word REVELATION.

In Saint-Martin next morning, the schoolmistress gave me papers stamped by the town hall, which made it possible for us to depart. Catherine got the car ready. All my willpower strained towards that departure. I hurried my friends. I pushed Catherine toward the car; she took the wheel; I sat between her and Michel. The car started. I was confident in the success of the journey, but terribly anguished, fearing difficulties which I thought inevitable. We were riding normally when, twenty kilometres beyond Saint-Martin, the car stopped; the brakes had jammed. I heard Catherine say: "The brakes have jammed." "Jammed!" I, too, was jammed within, by forces foreign to my conscious will, which were also paralyzing the mechanism of the car. This was the first stage of my identification with the external world. I was the car. The car had jammed on account of me, because I, too, was jammed between Saint-Martin and Spain. I was horrified by my own power. At that time, I was still limited to my own solar system, and was not aware of other people's systems, the importance of which I realise now.

We had driven all night long. I would see before me, on the road, trucks with legs and arms dangling behind them, but being unsure of myself, I would say shyly: "There are trucks ahead of us," just to find out what the answer would be. When they said: "The road is wide, we'll manage to bypass them," I felt reassured; but I did not know whether or not they saw what was carried in those trucks, greatly fearing I would arouse their suspicions and becoming prey to shame, which paralysed me. The road was lined with rows of coffins, but I could find no pretext to draw their attention to this embarrassing subject. They obviously were people who had been killed by the Germans. I was very frightened: *it all stank of death.* I learned later that there was a huge military cemetery in Perpignan.

In Perpignan, at seven in the morning, there were no rooms in the hotels. My friends had left me in a café; from then on, I had no rest: I was convinced I was responsible for my friends. I believed that it was useless to call on the higher authorities if we wanted to cross the border, and I sought instead the advice of bootblacks, café waiters, and passersby who I thought were vested with tremendous power.

We were to meet, at a point two kilometres distant from Andorra, with two Andorrans who were supposed to get us across the border in exchange for the gift of our car. Catherine and Michel told me very seriously that I had better refrain from talking. I agreed and dived into a voluntary coma.

When we reached Andorra, I could not walk straight. I walked like a crab; I had lost control over my motions: an attempt at climbing stairs would again bring about a "jam."

In Andorra—a deserted and godforsaken country—we were the first refugees to be received in the Hôtel de France by a little maidservant who bore the entire responsibility for that strangely empty establishment.

My first steps in Andorra meant to me what the first steps on a tightrope must mean to an acrobat. At night, my exasperated nerves imitated the noise of the river, which flowed tirelessly over some rocks: hypnotizing, monotonous.

By day, we tried to walk about on the mountainside, but no sooner would I attempt to ascend the slightest slope than I would jam like Catherine's Fiat, and be compelled to climb down again. My anguish jammed me completely.

I realized that my anguish—my mind, if you prefer—was painfully trying to unite itself with my body; my mind could no longer manifest itself without producing an immediate effect on my body—on matter. Later it would exercise itself upon other objects. I was trying to understand this vertigo of mine: that my body no longer obeyed the formulas established in my mind, the formulas of old, limited Reason; that my will no longer meshed with my faculties of movement, and since my will no longer possessed any power, it was necessary first to liquidate my paralyzing anguish, then to seek an accord between the mountain, my mind, and my body. In order to be able to move around in this new world, I had recourse to my heritage of British diplomacy and set aside the strength of my will, seeking through gentleness an understanding between the mountain, my body, and my mind.

One day I went to the mountain alone. At first I could not climb; I lay flat on my face on the slope with the sensation that I was being completely absorbed by the earth. When I took the first steps up the slope, I had the physical sensation of walking with tremendous effort in some matter as thick as mud. Gradually, however, perceptibly and visibly, it all became easier, and in a few days I was able to negotiate jumps. I could climb vertical walls as easily as any goat. I very seldom got hurt, and I realised the possibility of a very subtle understanding which I had not perceived before. Finally, I managed to take no false steps and to wander around quite easily among the rocks.

It is obvious that, for the ordinary citzen, this must have taken on a strange and crazy aspect: a well-brought-up young Englishwoman jumping from one rock to another, amusing herself in so irrational a manner: this was wont to raise immediate suspicions as to my mental balance. I gave little thought to the effect my experiments might have on the humans by whom I was surrounded, and, in the end, they won.

Following my pact with the mountain—once I could move easily in the most forbidding places—I proposed to myself an agreement with the animals: horses, goats, birds. This was accomplished through the skin, by means of a sort of "touch" language, which I find difficult to describe now that my senses have lost the acuity of perception they possessed at the time. The fact remains that I could draw near animals where other human beings put them to precipitate flight. During a walk with Michel and Catherine, for instance, I ran forward to join a herd of horses. I was exchanging caresses with them when the arrival of Catherine and Michel caused them to scamper away.

All of this was taking place in June and July, and

the refugees were piling up. Michel sent wire upon wire to my father in an effort to secure visas for Spain. Finally a curé brought a mysterious and very dirty piece of paper, coming from I know not what agent of my father's business connection, ICI (Imperial Chemicals), which should have allowed us to resume our journey. Twice already we had attempted to cross the Spanish border: the third attempt proved successful, thanks to the curé's bit of paper. Catherine and I reached Seo de Urgel. Unfortunately, Michel was unable to come over. The two of us then drove in the Fiat to Barcelona.

I was quite overwhelmed by my entry into Spain: I thought it was my kingdom; that the red earth was the dried blood of the Civil War. I was choked by the dead, by their thick presence in that lacerated countryside. I was in a great state of exaltation when we arrived in Barcelona that evening, convinced that we had to reach Madrid as speedily as possible. I therefore prevailed upon Catherine to leave the Fiat in Barcelona; the next day we boarded a train for Madrid.

The fact that I had to speak a language I was not acquainted with was crucial: I was not hindered by a preconceived idea of the words, and I but half understood their modern meaning. This made it possible for me to invest the most ordinary phrases with a hermetic significance.

In Madrid, we put up at the Hotel Internacional, near the railway station, leaving it later for the Hotel Roma. At the Internacional we dined that first night on the roof; to be on a roof answered for me a profound need, for there I found myself in a euphoric state. In the political confusion and the torrid heat, I convinced myself that Madrid was the world's stomach and that I had been chosen for the task of restoring this digestive organ to health. I believed that all anguish had accumulated in me and would dissolve in the end, and this explained to me the force of my emotions. I believed that I was capable of bearing this dreadful weight and of drawing from it a solution for the world. The dysentery I suffered from later was nothing but the *illness* of Madrid taking shape in my intestinal tract.

A few days later, in the Hotel Roma, I met a Dutch man, Van Ghent, who was Jewish and somehow connected with the Nazi government, who had a son working for Imperial Chemicals, the English company. He showed me his passport, infested with Swastikas. More than ever I aspired to ridding myself of all social constraints; to that end, I made a present of my papers to an unknown person and tried to give Max's passport to Van Ghent, but he refused to take it.

This scene took place in my room; the man's gaze was as painful to me as if he had thrust pins into my eyes. When he refused to take Max's passport, I remember that I replied: "Ah! I understand, I must kill him myself," i.e., disconnect myself from Max.

Not content with giving my papers away, I felt obliged to strip myself of everything. One evening, as I sat by Van Ghent on a café terrace watching the people of Madrid passing by, I felt that they were being manipulated by his eyes. At that moment, he pointed out to me that I was no longer wearing a small brooch I had purchased a few moments before as a badge of the sorrows of Madrid. Then he added: "Look in your handbag and you will find it there." True enough, the badge was there. To me this was a further proof of Van Ghent's nefarious power. Disgusted, I rose to my feet and entered the café, with the firm intention of distributing everything I carried in my bag to the officers who were there. Not one of them would accept. It seems to me that this whole scene took place in a very short time; however I suddenly found myself alone with a group of Requeté officers. Van Ghent had disappeared. Some of the men rose and pushed me into a car. Later, I was in front of a house, the windows of which were adorned with wrought-iron balconies, in the Spanish style. They showed me into a room decorated in Chinese style, threw me onto a bed, and after tearing off my clothes raped me one after the other.

I put up such a fight that they finally grew tired and let me get up. While I was trying to adjust my clothes in front of a mirror, I saw one of them open my bag and remove all of its contents. This action seemed absolutely normal to me, as did his sousing my head with a bottleful of eau de cologne.

This done, they took me somewhere near El Retiro, the big park, where I wandered about, lost, my clothes torn. Finally I was picked up by a policeman, who took me back to the hotel, where I telephoned Van Ghent, who was asleep—it was perhaps three o'clock in the morning. I thought that my story would change his attitude towards the people of the earth, but he became furious, insulted me, and hung up. I went up to my room and found on my bed some nightgowns belonging to Catherine, which the laundress had deposited there by mistake. I imagined that Van Ghent, acknowledging my power, had made amends and sent them to me as a present. It seemed indispensable to me to try on these nightgowns immediately. I spent the rest of the night taking cold baths and putting on nightgowns, one after the other. One was of pale green silk, another pink.

I was still convinced that it was Van Ghent who had hypnotized Madrid, its men and its traffic, he who turned the people into zombies and scattered anguish like pieces of poisoned candy in order to make slaves of all. One night, having torn up and scattered in the streets a vast quantity of newspapers which I believed to be a hypnotic device resorted to by Van Ghent, I stood at the door of the hotel, horrified to see people in the Alameda go by who seemed to be made of wood. I rushed to the roof of the hotel and wept, looking at the chained city below my feet, the city it was my duty to liberate. Coming down to Catherine's room, I begged her to look at my face; I said to her: "Don't you see that it is the exact representation of the world?" She refused to listen to me and put me out of her room.

Coming down into the lobby of the hotel, I found there, among other people, Van Ghent and his son, who accused me of madness, obscenity, etc.; no doubt they were frightened by my afternoon exploit with the newspapers. Thereupon I ran to the public garden and played there for a few moments in the grass, to the amazement of all passersby. An officer of the Falange brought me back to the hotel, where I spent the night bathing over and over again in cold water.

To me Van Ghent was my father, my enemy, and the enemy of mankind; I was the only one who could vanquish him; to vanquish him it was necessary for me to understand him. He gave me cigarettes—they were pretty scarce in Madrid—and one morning when I was particularly excited, it dawned on me that my condition was not solely due to natural causes and that his cigarettes were doped. The logical conclusion of this idea was to report Van Ghent's horrible power to the authorities and then proceed to liberate Madrid. An accord between Spain and England seemed to me the best solution. I therefore called at the British Embassy and saw the Consul there. I endeavored to convince him that the World War was being waged hypnotically by a group of people—Hitler and Co.—who were represented in Spain by Van Ghent; that to vanquish him it would suffice to understand his hypnotic power; we would then stop the war and liberate the world, which was "jammed," like me and Catherine's Fiat; that instead of wandering aimlessly in political and economic labyrinths, it was essential to believe in our metaphysical force and divide it among all human beings, who would thus be liberated. This good British citizen perceived at once that I was mad, and phoned a physician, Martínez Alonzo by name, who, once he had been informed of my political theories, agreed with him.

That day, my freedom came to an end. I was locked up in a hotel room, in the Ritz. I felt perfectly content; I washed my clothes and manufactured various ceremonial garments out of bath towels in preparation for my visit to Franco, the first person to be liberated from his hypnotic somnambulism. As soon as he was liberated, Franco would come to an understanding with England, then England with Germany, etc. Meanwhile, Martínez Alonzo, thoroughly puzzled by my condition, fed me bromide by the quart and begged me repeatedly not to remain naked when waiters brought me my food. He was panic-stricken and stultified by my political theories, and after a fifteen-day calvary, he withdrew to a seaside resort in Portugal, leaving me in the care of a physician-friend of his, Alberto N.

Alberto was handsome; I hastened to seduce him, for I said to myself: "Here is my brother, who has come to liberate me from the *fathers*." I had not enjoyed love since Max's departure and I wanted to very badly. Unfortunately Alberto, too, was a perfect fool and probably a scoundrel besides. In truth, I believe he was attracted to me, all the more so as he was aware of the power of Papa Carrington and his millions, as represented in Madrid by the ICI. Alberto would take me out, and once more I enjoyed some sort of temporary freedom. But not for long.

I called every day on the head of the ICI in Madrid; he soon got tired of my visits, most of all because I came to enlighten him on politics and denounced him, pell-mell with Papa Carrington and Van Ghent, as being petty, very petty, and pretty ignoble; and this to himself, his wife, his maids, the hotel servants, and anyone who would listen to me. He summoned a certain Dr. Pardo and encouraged me to enlighten him on the affairs of the world. I soon found myself a prisoner in a sanitorium full of nuns. This did not last long either; the nuns proved unable to cope with me. It was impossible to lock me up, keys and windows were no obstacles for me; I wandered all over the place, looking for the roof, which I believed my proper dwelling place.

After two or three days, the head of the ICI told me that Pardo and Alberto would take me to a beach at San Sebastián, where I would be absolutely free. I came out of the nursing home and got into a car bound for Santander. . . . On the way, I was given Luminal three times and an injection in the spine: systemic anesthesia. And I was handed over like a cadaver to Dr. Morales, in Santander.

Tuesday, August 24, 1943

I am afraid I am going to drift into fiction, truthful but incomplete, for lack of some details which I cannot conjure up today and which might have enlightened us. This morning, the idea of the egg came again to my mind and I thought that I could use it as a crystal to look at Madrid in those days of July and August 1940—for why should it not enclose my own experiences as well as the past and future history of the Universe? The egg is the macrocosm and the microcosm, the dividing line between the Big and the Small which makes it impossible to see the whole. To possess a telescope without its other essential half—the microscope—seems to me a symbol of the darkest incomprehension. The task of the right eye is to peer into the telescope, while the left eye peers into the microscope.

In Madrid, I had not yet known suffering "in its essence"; I wandered into the unknown with the abandon and courage of ignorance. When I gazed at posters in the streets, I saw not only the commercial and beneficent qualities of Mr. X's canned goods but hermetic answers to my queries as well—when I read AZAMON COMPANY or IMPERIAL CHEMICALS, I also read CHEMISTRY AND ALCHEMY, a secret telegram addressed to myself in the guise of a manufacturer of agricultural machinery. When the telephone rang or fell silent, answering or refusing to answer me, it was the inner voice of the hypnotized people of Madrid (there is no symbol hidden here, I am speaking literally). When seated at a table with other people in the lobby of the Hotel Roma, I heard the vibrations of beings as clearly as voices—I understood from each particular vibration the attitude of each towards life, his degree of power, and his kindness or malevolence towards me. It was no longer necessary to translate noises, physical contacts, or sensations into rational terms or words. I understood every language in its particular domain: noises, sensations, colours, forms, etc., and every one found a twin correspondence in me and gave me a perfect answer. As I listened to the vibrations, with my back to the door, I knew perfectly whether Catherine, Michel, Van Ghent, or his son was entering the dining room. As I looked into eyes, I knew the masters and the slaves and the (few) free men.

I worshipped myself in such moments. I worshipped myself because I saw myself complete—I was all, all was in me; I rejoiced at seeing my eyes become miraculously solar systems, kindled by their own light; my movements, a vast and free dance, in which everything was ideally mirrored by every gesture, a limpid and faithful dance; my intestines, which vibrated in accord with Madrid's painful digestion, satisfied me just as much. At that time, Madrid was singing *"Los ojos verdes"* (The Green Eyes), after a poem by, I think, García Lorca. Green eyes had always been for me my brother's, and now they were those of Michel, of Alberto, and of a young man from Buenos Aires whom I had met in the train between Barcelona and Madrid. . . . Green eyes, the eyes of my brothers who would deliver me at last of my father. I was obsessed by two other songs: *"El barco velero"* (The Sailboat), which was to take me to the Unknown, and *"Bei mir bist du schön,"* which was sung in every language and which, I thought, was telling me to make peace on earth.

I ceased menstruating at that time, a function which was to reappear but three months later, in Santander. I was transforming my blood into comprehensive energy—masculine and feminine, microcosmic and macrocosmic—and into a wine that was drunk by the moon and the sun.

I now must resume my story at the moment I came out of the anesthesia (sometime between the nineteenth and twenty-fifth of August 1940). I woke up in a tiny room with no windows on the outside, the only window being pierced into the wall to the right that separated me from the next room. In the left corner, facing my bed, stood a cheap wardrobe of varnished pine; to my right, a night table in the same style, with a marble top, a small drawer, and, underneath, an empty space for the chamber pot; also a chair; near the night table was a door which, I was to learn later, led to the bathroom; facing me, a glass door gave onto a corridor and onto another door panelled with opaque glass, which I watched avidly because it was clear and luminous and I guessed that it opened into a room flooded with sunshine.

My first awakening to consciousness was painful: I thought myself the victim of an automobile accident; the place was suggestive of a hospital, and I was being watched by a repulsive-looking nurse who looked like an enormous bottle of Lysol. I was in pain, and I realised that my hands and feet were bound by leather straps. I learned later that I had entered that place fighting like a tigress, that on the evening of my arrival Don Mariano, the physician who was head of the sanitorium, had tried to induce me to eat and that I had clawed him. He had slapped and strapped me down and compelled me to absorb food through tubes inserted into my nostrils. I don't remember anything about it.

I tried to understand where I was and why I was there. Was it a hospital or a concentration camp? I asked the nurse questions, which were probably incoherent; she gave me richly negative answers in English with a very disagreeable American accent. Later I learned that her name was Asegurado (or "insured," in the commercial sense of the word), that she was German, from Hamburg, and had lived for a long time in New York.

I never was able to discover how long I had remained unconscious: days or weeks? When I became sadly reasonable, I was told that for several days I had acted like various animals—jumping up on the wardrobe with the agility of a monkey, scratching, roaring like a lion, whinnying, barking, etc.

Held by the leather straps, I said very politely to Frau Asegurado: "Untie me, please." She said mistrustfully: "Will you be good?" I was so surprised by her question that I remained disconcerted for a few moments and could not produce an answer. I had only meant to do good to the entire world, and here I was, tied down like a wild beast! I could not understand, I had no memory whatsoever of my violent outbursts, and it all seemed to be a stupid injustice which I could only explain by blaming it on some Machiavellian impulse on the part of my guardians.

I asked: "Where is Alberto?"

"He is gone."

"Gone?"

"Yes, gone to Madrid."

Alberto gone to Madrid . . . impossible! "Where are we here—far from Madrid?"

"Very far. . . ."

And so on. I felt that I was drifting further and further away as the conversation went on, finally to find myself in some unknown and hostile country. She then told me that I was here for a rest. . . . For a rest! Finally, by dint of gentleness and very subtle arguments, I persuaded her to unstrap me and I dressed, full of curiosity for what lay outside the room. I walked along the corridor without attempting to open the door with the opaque glass panels, and reached a small square hall with windows closely corseted with iron bars. I thought: A funny rest place! These bars are here to prevent me from going out. I will come close to that iron and convince it to give my freedom back to me.

I was studying the matter closely, hanging batwise from the bars with my feet, my back turned to the room, and I was examining the bars on all sides, from all angles, when someone jumped on me. Falling miraculously back on my feet, I found myself face to face with an individual with the expression and aspect of a mongrel dog. I learned later that he was a congenital idiot who boarded at Dr. Morales's. Being a charity case, he served as a watchdog at Villa Covadonga, a pavilion for the dangerously and incurably insane named after Don Mariano's daughter who died. I realised that any discussion with such a creature was perfectly useless. I therefore took prompt measures to annihilate him. Frau Asegurado watched the battle from the vantage point of an armchair.

I was superior to my adversary in strength, willpower, and strategy. The idiot ran away weeping, covered with blood and terribly punished with scratches. I was told later that he would have submitted to death rather than come near me after that fight.

After I had explained a thousand times that I only wanted to see the garden, Frau Asegurado finally consented to accompany me outside. The garden was very green despite the tufts of bluish vapor of the tall eucalyptus trees; before Covadonga lay an orchard of apple-laden trees. I realized that autumn had come and, the sun being low, that evening was drawing near.

I probably was still in Spain. The vegetation was European, the climate soft, the architecture of Covadonga rather Spanish. But I was not at all sure of this, and seeing later the strange morality and conduct of the people who surrounded me, I felt still more at sea, and ended believing that I was in another world, another epoch, another civilisation, perhaps on another planet containing the past and future and, simultaneously, the present.

My keeper always wanted me to sit on a chair like a good girl. I refused, because I simply had to solve "the problem" as quickly as possible. When I walked to the right or left, she would follow me. Finally I sat down under a bower and a young man dressed in a blue smock—José—appeared suddenly and watched me with interest. I was relieved when I heard him speak Spanish. So I was in Spain! I found him handsome and attractive. He and Frau Asegurado followed me when I walked towards Villa Pilar to examine that pavilion. (By looking at the map, you will see the respective positions of Villa Pilar, Radiografía, Covadonga, Amachu, and Abajo (Down Below); that will enable you to get your bearings.) It was a grey stone building with iron-barred windows. To my utter surprise someone, hiding behind the bars, yelled at me from the first storey: "Leonora! Leonora!"

I was overcome. "Who are you?"

"Alberto!"

Alberto! So he was there! I wondered how I could manage to rejoin him, but the half-hidden face I glimpsed was hideous and deformed. As a matter of fact this was a practical joke of the nurses, who had suggested it to a madman by the name of Alberto. Yet I was pleased by this incident, believing that I had been followed by Al-

Portrait of Dr. Morales

berto, that I had not been betrayed by him, and that he was a prisoner like me.

I jumped with joy among the apple trees, sensing again the strength, the suppleness and beauty of my body. Soon a very short nurse, Mercedes, appeared in the alley running at top speed, followed by Moro, a black dog; behind her came, at a more leisurely pace, a tall fat man, also dressed in white. I recognized in him a powerful being and hastened to meet him, saying to myself: "This man holds the solution of the problem." When I drew near, I was disagreeably impressed: I saw that his eyes were like Van Ghent's, only still more terrifying. I thought: He belongs to the same gang and is possessed like the others, be careful! He was Don Luis Morales, Don Mariano's son.

Although I had approached just out of reach of his hands, he tried to grab me. I avoided his touching me, while staying close. At that moment José appeared and seized me. I defended myself honourably till another man came up—Santos—and joined in the fray. Don Luis had seated himself comfortably between two tree roots and enjoyed the show as the two men, José and Santos, threw me on the ground. José sat on my head and Santos and Asegurado tried to fasten down my arms and legs, which kept thrashing around. Armed with a syringe that she wielded like a sword, Mercedes stuck a needle into my thigh.

I thought it was a soporific and decided not to sleep. To my great surprise, I did not get sleepy. I saw my thigh swell around the puncture, till the bump grew to the size of a small melon.

Frau Asegurado told me they had induced an artificial abscess in my thigh; the pain and the idea that I was infected made it impossible for me to walk freely for two months. As soon as they loosened their grip, I threw myself furiously against Don Luis. I drew his blood out with my nails before José and Santos had a chance to drag me away. Santos choked me with his fingers.

At Covadonga, they tore my clothes off brutally and strapped me naked to the bed. Don Luis came into my room to gaze upon me. I wept copiously and asked him why I was kept a prisoner and treated so badly. He left quickly without answering me. Then Frau Asegurado appeared once more. I asked her several questions. She said to me: "It is necessary that you should know who Don Luis is; every night he comes and talks to you; standing on your bed, you answer him according to his will." I did not remember any of this. I swore to myself that, from that moment on, I would remain watchful day and night, that I would never sleep and would protect my consciousness.

I don't know how long I remained bound and naked. Several days and nights, lying in my own excrement, urine, and sweat, tortured by mosquitoes whose stings made my body hideous—I believed that they were the spirits of all the crushed Spaniards who blamed me for my internment, my lack of intelligence, and my submissiveness. The extent of my remorse rendered their assaults bearable. I was not greatly inconvenienced by the filth.

In the daytime, I was watched over by Frau Asegurado; at night, by José or Santos. From time to time, José would put his cigarette in my mouth so that I could inhale a few puffs of tobacco smoke; once in a while he would wipe my body, which was always burning hot, with a moist towel. I was grateful to him for his care. A squinting maidservant (they called her Piadosa) brought me my food: vegetables and raw eggs, which she introduced into my mouth with a spoon, taking good care not to be bitten. I was fond of her and *I would not have bitten her*. I thought that Piadosa, which means pious, meant painful feet, and I felt sorry for her because she had walked so much.

At night especially I would study my situation. I examined the straps with which I was bound, the objects and the persons by whom I was surrounded, and myself. An immense swelling paralysed my left thigh, and I knew that by freeing my left hand, I could cure myself. My hands are always cold and the heat of my leg *had* to melt under the coolness of my hand, the pain and the swelling would disappear. I don't know how, but I did manage to achieve this sometime later, and soon both the pain and the inflammation subsided, as I had foreseen.

One night, as I lay awake, I had a dream: a bedroom, huge as a theatrical stage, a vaulted ceiling painted to look like a sky, all of it very ramshackle but luxurious, an ancient bed provided with torn curtains and cupids, painted or real, I no longer know which; a garden very much like the one in which I had strolled the day before; it was surrounded by barbed wire over which my hands had made plants grow, plants which twisted themselves around the strands of wire and, covering them, hid them from sight.

The day after I had that vision, Don Luis came and spoke to me. I meant to ask him for a bandage for my thigh, but this immediately went out of my head. I also meant to ask him where Alberto was, but that also escaped from my mind and I found myself, unwittingly, in the midst of a political discussion. While I talked, I was surprised to find myself once more in a garden similar to the one I had dreamt about. We were sitting on a bench in the sunshine and I was neat and dressed; I was happy and lucid, I was saying, among other things: "I can do anything, thanks to Knowledge." He answered: "In that case, make me the greatest physician in the world."

"Give me my freedom, and you shall be."

I also said: "Outside this garden, so green and so fertile, there is an arid landscape; to the left, a mountain on top of which stands a Druidic temple. That temple, poor and in ruins, is my temple, it was built for me, also poor and in ruins; containing only some dry wood, it will be the place where I shall live, calling on you every day; then I shall teach you my Knowledge."

This was the exact meaning of my words. However, when I was allowed later to go out, I found no such temple and the countryside was altogether fertile.

The memory of Alberto and of my thigh suddenly came back to my mind. I at once found myself naked, miserable, and dirty on my bed, and Don Luis stood up to leave.

After that conversation, I sent him, through José, a triangle drawn on a piece of paper (I had had great difficulties obtaining pencil, paper, and permission to free my hands to draw it). That triangle, to my way of thinking, explained everything.

Wednesday, August 25, 1943

I have been writing for three days, though I had expected to deliver myself in a few hours; this is painful, because I am living this period all over again and sleeping badly, troubled and anxious as I am about the usefulness of what I am doing. However, I must go on with my story in order to come out of my anguish. My ancestors, malevolent and smug, are trying to frighten me.

During the whole time I was tightly tied to my bed, I had an opportunity to get acquainted with my strange neighbours; a knowledge which did not help me solve my problem, to wit: Where was I and why was I there? They came and watched me through the glass panel in my door. Sometimes they would come in and talk to me: the Prince of Monaco and Pan America, Don Antonio with his matchbox containing a small piece of excrement, Don Gonzalo pursued and tortured by the Archbishop of Santander, the Marquis da Silva with his giant spiders—he was drying out from a heroin addiction (he was also suffering from the same injection that had been given me, though the nurses claimed the swelling came from a spider bite)—who had been the intimate friend of Alfonso XIII, and was also Franco's friend. The Marquis was powerful in the Requeté, the Carlist Party; he was very nice and gaga.

Observing in those gentlemen a certain extravagance, I inferred that they were all under the hypnotic influence of Van Ghent's gang and that this place was consequently some sort of prison for those who had threatened the power of that group; also that I, the most dangerous of all, was fated to undergo a still more terrible torture in order to be reduced better still and become like my companions in distress.

I thought that the Moraleses were masters of the Universe, powerful magicians who made use of their power to spread horror and terror. I knew by dint of divination that the world was congealed, that it was up to me to vanquish the Moraleses and the Van Ghents in order to set it in motion again.

After several days of enforced immobility, I noticed that my brain was still functioning and that I was not defeated; I believed that my cerebral power was superior to my enemies'.

One evening, as I was being watched over by José and Mercedes, I suddenly felt horribly depressed. I felt that I was being possessed by Don Luis's mind, that his domination was swelling within me like a giant automobile tyre, and I heard his vast and immense desire to *crush* the Universe. I was penetrated by all of this as by a foreign body. This was torture. I was convinced at this moment that Don Luis was absent (which was true) and I had but one idea: to profit by his absence to escape the unclean power of his being. He had given me his power, convinced that I could not contain it, sure that he was my antipode, sure that he could kill me just like an intravenous injection of some virulent poison. Weeping, I begged José and Mercedes to unstrap me and come with me to Madrid, far from this terrible man. They answered: "But it would not be practical to leave for Madrid naked!" José however unstrapped me, and I prepared my luggage (a very dirty bed sheet and a pencil) while reciting: "Liberty, Equality, Fraternity." I walked painfully as far as the vestibule, followed by my little cortege. My left leg was horribly painful.

Don Luis returned at that moment. I heard his car—and he entered, accompanied by two men, one of whom was supposedly a Mexican upon whom I later avenged myself in Portugal. I don't remember who the other one was.

I don't know how long we all stood there transfixed—I thought I was holding them still with my eyes. The Mexican was laughing, the others were petrified. It was Don Luis, I believe, who finally broke the spell. My attention having faltered for one second, José and Mercedes threw themselves upon me and dragged me forcibly to my room. A hellish half hour followed: I held José and Mercedes by their hands and could not let them go: we were stuck to each other by some overpowering force, no one could speak or move. By an effort of will I managed to detach my hands from theirs; everyone then set to talking at a terrifying rate of speed. Whenever I would get hold of their hands once more, silence reigned immediately and our glances would once more be riveted to each other. This lasted perhaps several hours. This seemed to me the result of an infernal joke on the part of Don Luis, whose purpose was to prove that if I wanted to fraternize with José and Mercedes, we would be physically joined together like Siamese twins, and that otherwise his power would take hold of me again to destroy me.

The next day must have been Sunday, for I still hear the sound of bells outside and the clatter of horses' hooves, which gave me a terrible nostalgia and a desire to run away. It seemed impossible to communicate with the outside world; I wondered who would help someone, dressed in a bed sheet and a pencil, to get to Madrid.

I had heard about several pavilions; the largest one was very luxurious, like a hotel, with telephones and unbarred windows; it was called Abajo (Down Below), and people lived there very happily. To reach that paradise, it was necessary to resort to mysterious means which I believed were the divination of the Whole Truth. I was meditating on the manner in which I could get there as rapidly as possible when I was warned by the arrival of Moro, the dog, of Don Luis's visit. His expression was so different from yesterday's that it seemed to me that the world had turned backwards; with the night, his usual self-possession had vanished; he was disheveled, dirty, agitated, and behaved like a madman. With the aid of José and Santos, he removed all the furniture from my room except for the bed, from which I watched his strange activity. I knew that my clothes and a few small objects belonging to me were under lock and key in the wardrobe they were taking away. Frau Asegurado stood impassively next to me. I thought that the day of spring cleaning had arrived, that it heralded my liberation, and I was filled with joy. But once they had completely emptied the room, they left without giving me the slightest explanation.

Frau Asegurado told me that Don Luis had gone mad. I heard a great commotion above my room, accompanied by yells and insults. The dog, Moro, stood by my bed motionless and stared at the ceiling. I thought that it was Moro who, at that moment, held the power, that Don Luis had given himself up to a fit of raving madness in order to take a vacation from himself. I saw Frau Asegurado as a telephone cable who transmitted the will of Don Luis (Frau Asegurado was the most motionless of women).

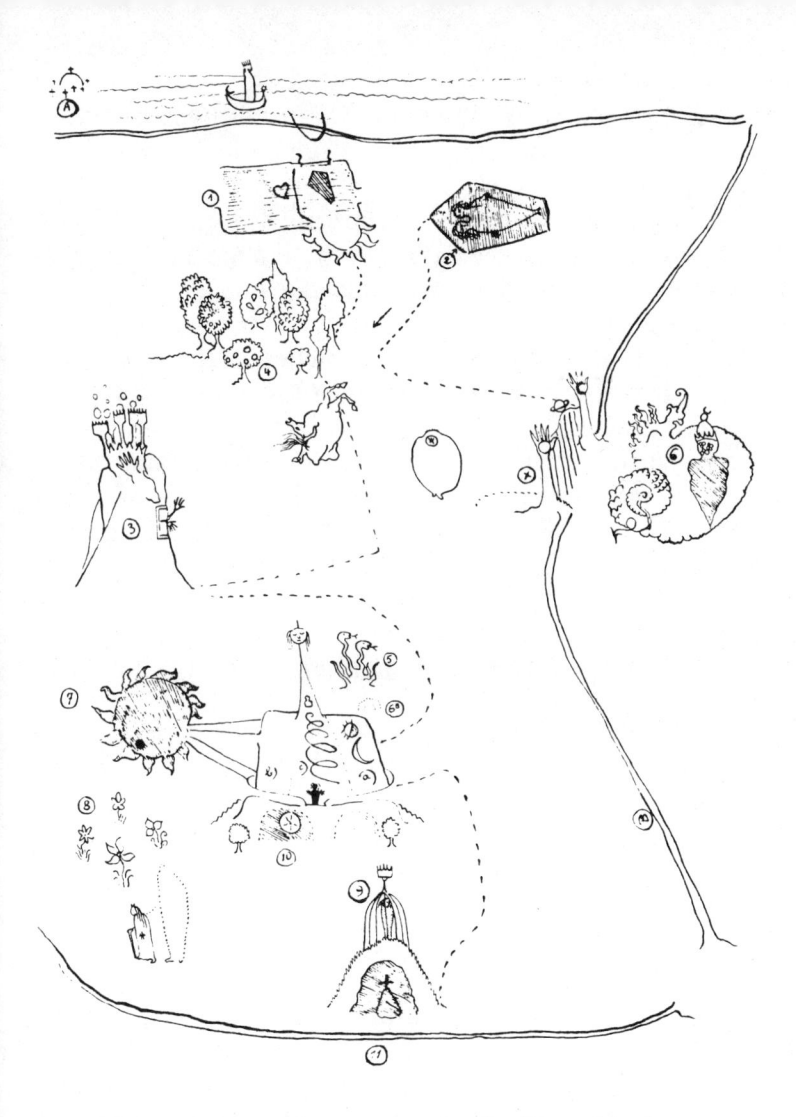

A.—A desert scene, Covagonda cemetery
B.—High wall surrounding the garden
X.—Gate of the garden
1.—Villa Covagonda
2.—Radiography
3.—Villa Pilar
4.—Apple trees and view of Casa Blanca and the valley
5.—"Africa".
6.—Villa Amachu
6B.—Arbor
7.—"Down Below"
8.—Kitchen garden
9.—Bower and cave
10.—Don Mariano's "place"
11.—"Outside World" Street
a.—My room at "Down Below," the eclipse and the limbos
b.—The lair
c.—The library
   Wide "Down Below" alley

I happened to be unstrapped that day, and from time to time I tried to escape, but Asegurado was watchful and I did not want to make use of violence against a woman for the sake of saving myself.

All day long the noise continued above my head, and I quietly rejoiced at the idea that Don Luis had become a raving maniac. Towards the end of that afternoon, the noise stopped suddenly and I heard steps on the stairs. I rushed into the hall, where a little old man appeared: it was Don Antonio with his matchbox, which still contained the sad little piece of excrement. I believed that Don Luis had sneaked into the old man's body: Don Antonio was not habitually violent and I have never been able to explain to myself the relentless noises of that strange Sunday.

After nightfall, Don Luis reappeared with a woman—Angelita: her street clothes, which were very neat, gave me some hope and I questioned her:

"You are a gypsy?" I asked.

"Yes."

"Where do you come from?"

"From Down Below."

"Is Down Below nice?"

"Delightful. Everyone is happy there."

"Take me with you."

"I can't."

"Why not?"

"Because you're not well enough to go there."

Thereupon Don Luis took me to the Sun Room, which was at that moment dark. I was entering that room for the first time. He began to talk about my visions, as though he had lived through them with me. Then he left suddenly; I wanted to follow him to Down Below with the gypsy, but Frau Asegurado prevented me and José came back to tie me down.

Later Piadosa got a bath ready for me. They bathed me for the first time that evening and cleaned my bed. I said to myself: "They are preparing my triumphal entry into Down Below." I believed they were purifying me in order to unite me with Alberto; I believed that the palace had been made ready to receive me; I believed this to be the dawn of freedom. Once I was left alone, clean in my bed, strapped as usual, the small window to the left lit up with such a beautiful warm orange light that I felt a delightful presence next to me. I was happy. Later José brought me his cigarette.

A new era began with the most terrible and blackest day in my life. How can I write this when I'm afraid to think about it? I am in terrible anguish, yet I cannot continue living alone with such a memory . . . I know that once I have written it down, I shall be delivered. But shall I be able to express with mere words the horror of that day?

The next morning, a stranger entered my room. He carried in his hand a physician's bag of black leather. He told me that he had come to take blood for a test and that he had to be helped by Don Luis. I replied that I was willing to receive one of them, but one at a time only, for I had noticed that the presence of more than one person in my room brought misfortune to me; moreover, that I was going to leave for Down Below and that I would not allow an injection to be given to me under any pretext. The discussion lasted for a pretty long time. It ended by my insulting him and he went away. Don Luis then entered and I announced my departure to him. Gentle and insinuating, he began talking about the blood taking. I spoke to him at length about my removal, about Alberto, and other things I don't remember. We spoke eye to eye; he was holding my left hand. All of a sudden, José, Santos, Mercedes, Asegurado, and Piadosa were in my room. Each one of them got hold of a portion of my body and I saw the *centre* of all eyes fixed upon me in a ghastly stare. Don Luis's eyes were tearing my brain apart and I was sinking down into a well . . . very far. . . . The bottom of that well was the stopping of my mind for all eternity in the essence of utter anguish.

With a convulsion of my vital center, I came up to the surface so quickly I had vertigo. Once more I saw the staring, ghastly eyes, and I howled: "I don't want . . . I don't want this unclean force. I would like to set you free but I won't be able to do so, because this astronomical force will destroy me if I don't crush you all . . . all . . . all. I must destroy you together with the whole world, because it is growing . . . it is growing, and the universe is not big enough for such a need of destruction. *I am growing. I am growing* . . . and I am afraid, because nothing will be left to destroy."

And I would sink again into panic, as if my prayer had been heard.

Have you an idea now of what the Great Epileptic Ailment is like? It's what Cardiazol induces. I learned later that my condition had lasted for ten minutes; I was convulsed, pitiably hideous, I grimaced and my grimaces were repeated all over my body.

When I came to I was lying naked on the floor. I shouted to Frau Asegurado to bring me some lemons and I swallowed them with their rinds. Only she and José were with me now. I rushed into the bathtub and splashed water all over me, on them both, on everything around me. Then I went back to bed, and tasted despair.

I confessed to myself that a being sufficiently powerful to inflict such a torture was stronger than I was; I admitted defeat, the defeat of myself and of the world around me, with no hope of liberation. I was dominated, ready to become the slave of the first comer, ready to die, it all mattered little to me. When Don Luis came to see me, later, I told him that I was the feeblest creature in the whole world, that I could meet his desires, whatever they were, and that I licked his shoes.

I must have slept for about twenty-four hours. I woke up in the morning; a little old man, dressed all in black, was watching me; I knew he was a *master* because the pinpoint pupils of his light eyes were similar to those of Van Ghent and Don Luis. This man was Don Mariano Morales. He spoke to me in French, very politely, something to which I was no longer accustomed.

"So you feel better, Mademoiselle? . . . I am no longer seeing a tigress, but a young lady."

He seemed to know me and I was expressing my surprise when Don Luis entered the room and said: "This is my father."

Don Mariano ordered that I be unstrapped and removed to the Sun Room in Covadonga. They could do what they pleased with me, I was as obedient as an ox.

The Sun Room was a pretty large room; one of its sides was made of opaque glass that gave out a dazzling light. Beatifically soaking in the muted sunshine, I felt as though I had left behind me the sordid and painful aspect of Matter and was entering a world which might have been the mathematical expression of Life. The room was furnished with a few chairs, a leather couch, and a small pinewood writing desk. The floor was covered with blue-and-white tiles. I lay down for hours in the light and contented myself with following the course of the sun through the glass panes. I took my food with docility and gave up resisting.

Thursday, August 26, 1943

It was, I am almost certain of it, the night before I was injected with Cardiazol that I had this vision:

The place looked like the Bois de Boulogne; I was on top of a small ridge bordered with trees; at a certain distance below me, on the road, stood a fence like those I had often seen at the Horse Show; next to me, two big horses were tied together; I was impatiently waiting for them to jump over the fence. After long hesitations, they jumped and galloped down the slope. Suddenly a small white horse detached himself from them; the two big horses disappeared, and nothing was left on the path but the colt, who rolled all the way down where he remained on his back, dying. *I myself was the white colt.*

The terrible downfall induced by Cardiazol was followed by several rather silent days. Around eight in the morning, I would hear from a distance the siren of a factory, and I knew this was the signal for Morales and Van Ghent to call the *zombies* to work and also to wake me, I who was entrusted with the task of liberating the day. Piadosa would enter then with a tray on which stood a glass of milk, a few biscuits, and some fruit. I took in this food according to a special ritual:

First, I would drink the milk at one draught, sitting bolt upright in my bed.

Second, I would eat the biscuits, half reclining.

Third, I would swallow all the fruit, lying down.

Fourth, I would put in a brief appearance in the bathroom, where I would observe that my food went through without being digested;

Fifth, back in my bed, I would sit up again very straight and examine the remnants of my fruit, rinds and stones, arranging them in the form of designs representing as many solutions to cosmic problems. I believed that Don Luis and his father, seeing the problems solved on my plate, would allow me to go Down Below, to Paradise.

Frau Asegurado would come in for my bath and then would take me to the Sun Room. Here I was rid of all my familiar objects which, belonging to the troubled and emotional past, would have darkened my labours. Here I was alone and naked, with my bed sheet and the sun— the sheet united to my body in a dance. Here in the Sun Room I felt I was manipulating the firmament: I had found what was essential to solving the problem of Myself in relation to the Sun.

I believed that I was being put through purifying tortures so that I might attain Absolute Knowledge, at which point I could live Down Below. The pavilion with this name was for me the Earth, the Real World, Paradise, Eden, Jerusalem. Don Luis and Don Mariano were God and His Son. I thought they were Jewish; I thought that I, a Celtic and Saxon Aryan, was undergoing my sufferings to avenge the Jews for the persecutions they were being subjected to. Later, with full lucidity, I would go Down Below, as the third person of the Trinity. I felt that, through the agency of the Sun, I was an androgyne, the Moon, the Holy Ghost, a gypsy, an acrobat, Leonora Carrington, and a woman. I was also destined to be, later, Elizabeth of England. I was she who revealed religions and bore on her shoulders the freedom and the sins of the earth changed into Knowledge, the union of Man and Woman with God and the Cosmos, all equal between them. The lump on my left thigh no longer seemed to form part of my body and became a sun on the left side of the moon; all my dances and gyrations in the Sun Room used that lump as a pivot. It was no longer painful, for I felt integrated into the Sun. My hands, Eve (the left one) and Adam (the right one), understood each other, and their skill was thereby increased tenfold.

With a few pieces of paper and a pencil José had given me, I made calculations and deduced that the father was the planet Cosmos, represented by the sign of the planet Saturn: ☺ The son was the Sun and I the Moon, an essential element of the Trinity, with a microscopic knowledge of the earth, its plants and creatures. I knew that Christ was dead and done for, and that I had to take His place, because the Trinity, minus a woman and microscopic knowledge, had become dry and incomplete. Christ was replaced by the Sun. I was Christ on earth in the person of the Holy Ghost.

Three days perhaps after my second Cardiazol injection, I was given back the objects which had been confiscated on my entering the sanatorium, and a few others besides. I realised that with the aid of these objects I had to set to work, combining solar systems to regulate the conduct of the World. I had a few French coins, which represented the downfall of men through their passion for money; those coins were supposed to enter into the planetary system as units and not as particular elements; should they join with other objects, wealth would no longer beget misfortune. My red-and-black refill pencil (leadless) was Intelligence. I had two bottles of eau de cologne: the flat one was the Jews, the other, cylindrical one, the non-Jews. A box of Tabu powder with a lid, half grey and half black, meant eclipse, complex, vanity, taboo, love. Two jars of face cream: the one with a black lid was night, the left side, the moon, woman, destruction; the other, with a green lid, was man, the brother, green eyes, the Sun, construction. My nail buff, shaped like a boat, evoked for me a journey into the Unknown, and also the talisman protecting that journey: the song *"El barco velero."* My little mirror was to win over the Whole. As for my Tangee lipstick, I have but a vague memory of its significance; it probably was the meeting with color and speech, painting and literature: Art.

Happy with my discovery, I would group these objects around each other; they wandered together on the celestial path, helping each other along and forming a complete rhythm. I gave an alchemical life to the objects according to their position and their contents. (My face cream Night, in the black-lidded jar, contained the lemon, which was an antidote to the seizure induced by Cardiazol.)

Lucid and gay, I waited impatiently for Don Luis. I said to myself: "I have solved the problems he set before me. I shall certainly be led Down Below." So I was horrified when, far from appreciating my labor, he gave me a second injection of Cardiazol.

Thereupon I organized my own defense. I knew that

by closing my eyes, I could avoid the advent of the most unbearable pain: the stare of others. Therefore I would keep them closed for a very, very long time at a stretch. This was my expiation for my exile from the rest of the world; this was the sign of my flight from Covadonga (which for me was Egypt) and of my return Down Below (Jerusalem), where I was destined to bring Knowledge; I had spent too much time putting up with the solitude of my own knowledge.

Keeping my eyes closed enabled me to endure the second Cardiazol ordeal much less badly, and I got up very quickly, saying to Frau Asegurado, "Dress me, I must go to Jerusalem to tell them what I have learned." She dressed me and I went into the garden, meeting no obstacle, Frau Asegurado behind me. I followed the alley, between the trees, leaving the apple trees and Villa Pilar to the right. As I advanced everything became richer and more beautiful around me. I did not stop until I came to the door of Down Below. An old woman, Doña Vicenta, sister of Don Mariano, was coming out of the house with a glass of water and a lemon, which she handed to me. I drank the water and kept the lemon as a talisman with which to carry out my perilous mission. I reached the foot of the stairs in my Paradise with a dreadful anguish, an anguish wholly comparable to the one I had experienced in front of the mountain, in Andorra. But, as in Andorra, I once again found the strength to struggle against the invisible powers that were striving to detain me, and I triumphed.

There were three storeys: in each a door was open. I could see in the rooms, on the night tables, other solar systems as perfect and complete as my own. *"Jerusalem knew already!"* They had penetrated the mystery at the same time as I. On the third floor, I came upon a small ogival door; it was closed; I knew that if I opened it, I would be in the center of the world. I opened it and saw a spiral staircase; I went up and found myself in a tower, a circular room lighted by five bull's-eye windows: one red, one green (the Earth and its plants), one translucent (the Earth and its men), one yellow (the Sun), and one mauve (the Moon, night, the future). A wooden column which served as an axis for this strange place jutted from the ceiling, passed through the center of a pentagonal table, which was laid with a small, torn red tablecloth, covered with dust. I took the great disorder which reigned on this table for the handiwork of God and of His Son: disorder among the various objects that were there, disorder in the cogs of the human machinery which, immobilized, kept the world in anguish, war, want, and ignorance.

I still can see those objects very distinctly: two stout pieces of wood cut out in the shape of an enlarged keyhole—a small pink box containing gold powder—a number of laboratory saucers of thick glass, some crescent shaped, others half-moon shaped, the remainder perfectly round (I seem to remember that some were triangular)—an oblong tin on which were pasted labels bearing the name of Franco and containing a morsel of dirt—lastly, a metal disk and a medal of Jesus Christ. Attached to the wall, so as to form a triangle in this circular room, hung three rectangular tanks of a metal I was unable to identify, they were so dirty on the outside, while inside they were covered with a thick layer of paint. The first was mauve, another pink; I don't remember the colour of the third. Each one was pierced through its side with a hole through which passed the handle of a large spoon.

I began by laying down the disk next to the column and by placing on top of it the two pieces of wood (male and female). I then poured all the gold dust over them, thus covering the world with riches. I then placed the saucers inside the tanks, and the Jesus Christ medal and the Franco box in my pocket. I opened all the windows, as I would have opened those of Consciousness, except for one: the mauve-coloured one, the Moon's, since my "moon cycle," my menstrual period, had stopped.

Having concluded the Work, I walked down the stairs and returned to "Egypt."

Friday, August 27, 1943

On the way to Covadonga, followed by Frau Asegurado, I met Don Mariano—God the Father, dressed as usual in his black robe, which was covered, at the level of his stomach, with a crust of old food dried over time. He was watching a very poor child who was picking up dry leaves and weeping. I asked what the child had done. Don Mariano answered: "He stole an apple from my orchard."

Outraged, I shouted at him: "You who possess so many apples! With such morality, no wonder the world is 'jammed' and miserable. But I have just broken your wicked spell in the tower, and now the world is liberated from its anguish."

The grandson of the Marquis da Silva went by at a run, and God the Father, reassured by the presence of such a "well-brought-up" child, smiled at him kindly.

I returned to Egypt, rather disgusted with the Holy Family. . . . From the bathroom window, I gazed for a long time at a sad, green landscape: flat fields stretching down to the sea; near the coast, a cemetery: the Unknown and Death.

I learned from Asegurado that Covadonga (Don Mariano's daughter) was buried in that cemetery. Frau Asegurado often spoke to me of Covadonga, surrounding her death with mystery; I believed that Don Luis had killed her through torture, to make her more perfect, as he had tortured me. I believed that Don Luis was seeking in me another sister who, stronger than Covadonga, would withstand her ordeals and reach *The Summit* with him. For this I was relying not on my strength but on my skill. I believed I had been mesmerised in Saint-Martin-d'Ardèche and drawn to Santander by some mysterious power.

One day Don Luis tried to get me to sketch a map of that journey. As I was unable to do so, he took the pencil from my hand and began to draw the itinerary. In the center he put down an *M* representing Madrid. At that moment I had my first flash of lucidity: the *M* was "Me" and not the whole world; this affair concerned myself alone, and if I could make the journey all over again, I would, by the time I reached Madrid, get hold of myself, would reestablish contact between my mind and my self.

Soon after my visit to Down Below, Don Luis decided to install me in Amachu; this was a pavilion outside the walls of the garden; there I would be alone with my servants. Why did I find myself "jammed" once more and in great anguish? Why did I imagine that I had been deemed unworthy to live in the Garden of Eden? After all, I was leaving behind me the sufferings endured in Egypt, in Covadonga.

The name of my new house—Amachu—and the fact it was a wooden building, made me think of China—halfway between Covadonga (Egypt) and Down Below (Jerusalem). I still had with me Piadosa, José, and Frau Asegurado; and Don Luis had told me that he did not believe it would be necessary to continue giving me Cardiazol. He had added: "This house will be your own, your home and you will be responsible for it." I, however, gave the word *home* a broader, cosmic meaning, which was represented by the number six.

Despite the confidence Don Luis had placed in me, despite the commonplace appearance of the small bungalow, which aroused no mistrust in my mind, I felt, upon entering the inner corridor that separated the various rooms, as though I was caught in a labyrinth, like a rat. The doors in the corridor looked as if they had been cut out of the wall and were part of it, and became almost invisible when closed. So here I was, confronted with a Chinese puzzle which I had to solve with the knowledge secured in Egypt.

One day Don Luis announced to me the visit of Nanny, who had been with me till my twentieth year. She arrived in great exaltation, after a terrible fifteen-day journey in the narrow cabin of a warship. She had not expected to find me in an insane asylum and thought she was going to see the healthy girl she had left four years ago. I received her coldly and mistrustfully: she was sent to me by my hostile parents, and I knew that her intention was to take me back to them. Upset by my attitude, Nanny became nervous. Frau Asegurado considered her arrival a regrettable event, though not dangerous for me. Nanny was mortified and horribly jealous because another woman had taken her place by my side. For me their jealousy became a cosmic problem, an almost impossible task that I had to solve, at Home, Amachu. When I left with Frau Asegurado for the big garden, I would give Nanny some task to keep her indoors. This happened every morning, at eleven, according to ritual.

    I would get ready to enter the gate of Paradise; from the threshold, we overlooked the entire estate and the valley; my joy was so complete that I would be compelled to halt for a few minutes and turn enraptured eyes toward a very green spot of grass where a small boy armed with a stick was watching over some cows. Then we would follow the wide alley leading to Down Below; we walked through a bower, in which I sat down; all around me was the Garden of Eden, to my left Don Luis's garage, where I always hoped to see him arrive. I would remain there, watchful and quiet, and allow Frau Asegurado to enter Down Below. She would come out a few moments later, laden with a tray on which stood a glass of milk, biscuits, honey, and a cigarette of blond tobacco: the food of the gods, which I savoured in ecstasy. I was beginning to get fatter. Then I would go into my dear Down Below; I would go straight across the hall to the library: this was a rectangular room furnished with a writing desk and a small bookcase. The room opened into two other rooms: one day when the door to the left stood ajar, I recognized the room from the vision I had had in Covadonga, a room with a vaulted ceiling, painted to represent the sky. Immediately I called it *my* room, the room of the Moon. The other room, the one to the right, was the room of the Sun, my Androgyne. I would sit at the desk after choosing a book by Unamuno in which he had written: "God be thanked: we have pen and ink." At that moment, Angelita, the Gypsy (in fact a nurse) who lived in Down Below, would bring me a pen and some paper. I would make out the horoscope of the day and entrust it to her, to give to Don Luis.

The library gave out onto a large terrace, where I would rest a moment. There, sitting above the Moraleses' dining room, I absorbed the atmosphere of Down Below. Then I would go down the stairs to the left, which led to the back part of the garden; on a mound stood a rather dilapidated bower; Frau Asegurado would bring me a chair and I would sit there, gazing at the valley over the iron gate, then set to work on the three figures which continually obsessed me: 6, 8, and 20; after lengthy calculations, I would get the figure 1600, which called to mind Queen Elizabeth . . . I thought at the time that I was her reincarnation. I would then come down from my bower and go around the mound, behind which a sort of cave had been dug for garden tools. Dead leaves were heaped there, and in my mind the heap took the shape of a tomb, which became for me Covadonga's and my own.

One day, on the path along the back of the garden, I met Don Luis and I asked him if he wanted to go to

China with me. He answered: "I do; but you mustn't say so to anybody, you talk too much. Learn to keep inside you the things that occupy your mind." (This was the signal for my first inhibition, my entry into hermetism.) Then he gave me a stick, which he called my Stick of Philosophy. It became a companion on all my walks. . . . Then I went into the garden, under the apple trees, and returned to Amachu in time for lunch.

In the evening, I would call on the Prince of Monaco, in Villa Pilar; we would listen together to Radio Andorra. I sat there happily as the Prince typed endless diplomatic letters at a furious rate. Whenever he stopped, we would exchange ideas with the utmost seriousness. His room was plastered with maps; the one that interested me particularly was a map of France and northern Spain on which my journey was traced in red pencil. I believed that the Prince was teaching me about my own journey.

Don Luis would call on me at midnight; his presence in my room at that hour inspired me with a desire for him. He talked to me gently and I believed he was coming to examine my delusions. Without waiting for his questions, I would say: "*I have no delusions*, I am playing. When will you stop playing with me?" He would stare at me in amazement at finding me lucid, then laugh. And I would say: "Who am I?" while thinking: Who am I *to you*?

He would leave without answering, completely disarmed.

In a moment of lucidity, I realised how necessary it was to extract from myself all the personages who were inhabiting me. But the determination to expel Elizabeth was the only need that remained with me: she was the character I disliked most of all. I conceived the idea of constructing her image in my room: a small, three-legged round table represented her legs; for a body, I placed a chair on top of the table and on that chair a decanter which represented her head. Into the decanter I stuck dahlias and yellow and red roses—Elizabeth's consciousness; then I dressed her up in my own clothes and placed on the floor, by the legs of the table, Frau Asegurado's shoes.

I had reconstructed this image so that it might leave me. I had to get rid of everything my illness had brought me, to cast out these personalities, and thus begin my liberation.

Happy with my success, I was on my way through the garden to Down Below when I noticed an enormous tuft of reeds which had grown in an old shell hole; spontaneously, I called the place Africa and set to gathering branches and leaves with which I completely covered myself. I returned to Amachu in a state of great sexual excitement. It seemed only natural to me to find Don Luis in my room, busy examining Elizabeth's dummy. I sat down next to him and he caressed my face and introduced his fingers gently into my mouth: This gave me real pleasure. Then he took my notebook and wrote down on one page: *"O Corte, o cortijo"* (You belong at court, or in a farmyard.) Whereupon I took to wanting him terribly, and to writing him every day.

One day at lunch I was upset by a nauseous smell in my room—they were spreading manure on the neighbouring fields. I could not understand why God the Father should tolerate that my meals be poisoned. Indignant, I rose from the table and, followed by Frau Asegurado, proceeded to find Don Mariano in his own dining room. Don Luis turned to my nurse and addressed her in German; irritated because I could not understand what he was saying, jealous because he was talking *to her* and not to me, I sat down between the two of them. I observed very clearheadedly that I was being run through by an electric current that went from the one to the other. To make sure I stood up, drew away from them, and felt immediately that the current had left my body. I knew that this current was the fluid of the fear they both had of me.

Don Mariano gave me his permission to move, and this is how I was admitted into Down Below. Frightened by the idea of living in the big garden, where she was afraid of meeting madmen, Nanny tried to dissuade me from installing myself Down Below. It was, she said, a dangerous and evil place. I insisted so much that she ended by yielding.

I arrived at last in the room with the vaulted ceiling, which I had seen in a vision at the beginning of my illness. The room was just as I had seen it, only smaller, and the painted ceiling was in fact flat, not vaulted; I entered there without emotion, almost with a sense of disappointment. I was examining the windows attentively, for I wanted to make sure that no microphones had been attached to them, when a large dragonfly entered and sat on my hand, its feet clinging to my skin. Its wings were trembling, it clung to me as if it would never again detach itself. I spent several minutes looking at it in this way, holding my hand motionless, until the dragonfly fell dead onto the tiles of the floor. . . .

That evening at dinnertime when I entered the circular dining room at Down Below, I was told that I could select my table; I realized that I had to find my place in the circle, and sat at 45 degrees to the left of the door, which seemed to me the place where I could best intercept all interesting currents in the room.

A few days later Don Luis proposed to me my first outing: we drove out in an automobile to pay some calls. We went to see a pregnant young lady to whom he had to give an injection (I believed it would be an injection of Cardiazol, and that I was the child she was bearing). She gave me a package of cigarettes and they left me alone in a dark drawing room. I rushed to the bookcase and found a Bible, which I opened at random. I happened on the passage in which the Holy Ghost descends upon the disciples and bestows upon them the power to speak all languages. I was the Holy Ghost and believed I was in limbo, my room—where the Moon and the Sun met at dawn and at twilight. When Don Luis came in, accompanied by the young lady, she spoke to me in German and I understood her, though I do not know the language. She gave me the Bible, which I pressed under my arm, eager to return home and hold my Stick of Philosophy, which Don Luis had not allowed me to take along.

When I entered the library of my pavilion, I found Nanny armed with my Stick. She needed it, she said, to defend herself against the demented inmates. How could she expect to put to such use my dear companion, my surest means of Knowledge? At that moment I hated her.

My second ride was in a horse carriage. Don Luis took me to the undertaker's, in Santander, where he rented me a carriage pulled by a small black horse. A very small boy sat down next to me, to keep me company. I drove the horse very fast and finally attained what felt like a dizzy speed, while the excited child cried out: "Faster! Faster!" In a wide avenue, we caught up with a company of soldiers who were singing: *"Ay, ay, ay, no te mires en el río"* (Don't look at yourself in the river). I returned, convinced that I had accomplished an act of the utmost importance.

One morning, Don Luis advised me to start reading. He gave Frau Asegurado a list of books and told her to take me to the bookstore. I was quiet and very happy before such a quantity of books, among which I expected to be allowed to choose freely. But I felt my hand reach in the opposite direction to the one I intended, and pick up books I had absolutely no desire to read. At that moment I noticed Frau Asegurado standing behind me; she felt to me like a *vacuum cleaner*. Every time I got a book off the shelves, I would consult the list, hoping that its title would not be there: but there I would find it every time. I begged her to leave my brain alone, demanded the freedom of my own will. I returned home in a rage. Frau Asegurado remained passive, unmoved, as if withdrawn from the scene. Don Luis showed up in my room immediately upon my return. I yelled at him: "I don't accept your force, the power of any of you, against me; I want my freedom to act and think; I hate and reject your hypnotic forces." He took me by the arm and led me to a pavilion which was not in use.

"I am the master here."

"I am not the public property of your house. I, too, have private thoughts and a private value. I don't belong to you."

And suddenly, I burst into tears. He took me by the arm, then, and I realised with horror that he was going to give me my third dose of Cardiazol. I promised him all that it was within my power to give if only he would desist from giving me the injection. On the way, I picked up a small eucalyptus fruit, in the belief that it would help me. He took me, vanquished, to the radiography pavilion. I resigned myself to take the place of his sister, to undergo the last ordeal, the one that would give him back Covadonga in my own person.

The room was papered with painted, silvery pine trees on a red background; a prey to the most complete panic, I saw pine trees in the snow. In the midst of convulsions, I relived my first injection, and felt again the atrocious experience of the original dose of Cardiazol: absence of motion, fixation, horrible reality. I did not want to close my eyes, thinking that the sacrificial moment had come and determined to oppose it with all my strength.

I was then taken to Down Below in a cataleptic state. Tirelessly, Nanny repeated, "What have they done to you . . . what have they done to you?" and wept by my bed, thinking that I was dead. But, far from being touched by her sorrow, I was exasperated by it, for I felt at that moment that my parents were still trying to pull me back through her. I drove her away; but from the next room, where one withdrew, I still suffered this suction of their will. I knew when she went away. At last I entered painlessly that state of prostration that usually follows this kind of treatment. Don Mariano was at my bedside when I woke up. He advised me not to return to my parents. At that moment, I regained my lucidity. My cosmic objects, my night creams and nail buff, had lost their significance.

It was at this time that Etchevarría appeared. I was sitting in the garden when another inmate, Don Gonzalo, advanced toward me and gave me a book from a man named Etchevarría, who sent apologies for being unable to bring it in person, as he was ill in bed that day. Two days later, I met in the library a small man with a grey face, wrapped in warm clothes. This was Etchevarría. He spoke amiably about my country. He sat down in the dining room at a table next to mine, then gazed at me for a long time, kindly, and said at last: "You will not remain here long."

A feeling of joy slowly grew within me: I was talking with a reasonable man who inspired no fear, who took me seriously and sympathetically. I spoke to him of my power over animals. He answered without a trace of irony: "Power over animals is a natural thing in a person as sensitive as you are." And I learned that Cardiazol was a simple injection and not an effect of hypnotism; that Don Luis was not a sorcerer but a scoundrel; that Covadonga and Amachu and Down Below were not Egypt, China, and Jerusalem, but pavilions for the insane and that I should get out as quickly as possible. He "demystified" the mystery which had enveloped me and which they all seemed to take pleasure in deepening around me.

After long conversations about desire, Etchevarría advised me to have sex with José. I ceased then being interested in Don Luis and began desiring José. I would meet him in various secluded spots of the garden and, spied on by Frau Asegurado and Mercedes, we would exchange quick and uncomfortable kisses. José was very fond of me. He plied me with cigarettes. . . .

He cried when I went away.

Postscript 1987

I had a cousin in Santander, in the other hospital, the big, ordinary hospital. He was a doctor, Guillermo Gil, and I think he was related to the Bamfords, my grandmother's family in Cheshire. He was half English and half Spanish. It was a coincidence. He arrived, and they didn't want anyone to see me. But he was a doctor and he insisted, and so I had an interview with him, and he said, "I'd like you to have tea with me. They can't refuse." Which they couldn't. And we chatted, and at the end, he said, "I'm going to write to the ambassador in Madrid, and get you out." Which he did. They sent me to Madrid with Frau Asegurado, my keeper.

It was New Year's Eve, I remember it very well. It was extremely cold, and we got held up in Ávila, where Santa Teresa was born. There was a long train with many trucks full of sheep, and they were all crying from the cold. It was awful, the Spanish can be so terrible with animals. I'll remember the suffering sheep to my dying day. It was like Hell. We were held up, I don't know why, for hours, listening to this absolutely hellish lament, and I was alone with Frau Asegurado.

Then we arrived in Madrid, and were staying in a large, rather expensive hotel. It is sort of tricky to talk about this period, because Imperial Chemicals were really up to all kinds of things. The man who ran it reappeared, and he was allowed to take me out to lunch, without Frau Asegurado, and sometimes in the evening too. One night, he and his wife had me to dinner, and they were afraid of me, because I'd just come out of the madhouse. I could see she was hesitating to give me a knife and fork. It was all I could do not to crack up, it was so funny. She was absolutely petrified of me; they both were. Then she didn't want to see me again. I was much too alarming to have around in the social life of Madrid.

One night it was very windy—this was winter, remember, and it's very cold in Madrid then—I went with him to a very expensive restaurant, and he said, "Your family have decided to send you to South Africa, to a sanatorium where you'll be very happy because it's so lovely there."

I said, "I'm not sure about that."

He added, "I have another idea, personal, of course: I could give you a lovely apartment here, and I could see you very very often." And he grabbed my thigh.

So I was then in front of a huge decision. Either I was shipped to South Africa, or I was going to bed with this appalling man. I quickly went to the lavatory. But I still hadn't decided when I came out. We were about to leave the restaurant when there was a tremendous gust of wind and the metal sign of the restaurant fell just in front of me, at my feet. It could have killed me, and so I turned around to him, and I said, "No. It's no." And that's all I said. I didn't have to say any more than that. "It's going to be Portugal and then South Africa for you then," he said.

They got everything ready to send me off, and Frau Asegurado went back to Santander. I was put on the train, with my papers, whatever they were. I'd given them all away but they seemed to turn up again. I was being shipped out. They were ashamed of me.

I was telling myself, "I'm not going to South Africa and another sanatorium!" Yet it didn't occur to me to get off the train before getting to Lisbon.

I descended in Lisbon, and was met by a committee from Imperial Chemicals—two men who looked like policemen, and a very very hard-faced woman. They said, "You're very lucky, you're going to live in a lovely house in Estoril, with Mrs. Whatever-Her-Name."

I'd learned by then, You don't fight with such people. You have to think more quickly than they. So I said, "That will be lovely."

We arrived in a house in Estoril, a few miles from Lisbon. There was barely a half inch of bathwater and a lot of parrots. I spent the night there and I did a bit of hard thinking, and the next day I said, "The weather's going to be terrible for my hands. I must have some gloves. And I haven't got a hat."

I was thinking, Get to Lisbon. It worked. She said, "Of course you must. Nobody goes out without gloves."

So off we went. We reached Lisbon, and I said to myself, "Now or never." I had to find a café that looked big enough, and then, "Aargh!" I cried, clutching my stomach. "Got to go to the bathroom." "Yes, immediately," she said. She conducted me inside. I had judged correctly: it was a café with two doors. I nipped out, got a taxi—I must have had a bit of money for buying the gloves—and I told the driver, in Spanish, "Mexican Embassy."

I'd met Renato Leduc, again, in Madrid. I'd run into

him at a thé dansant. I was allowed to watch the other people dancing, though I wasn't allowed to dance, of course. I was with my keeper, Frau Asegurado—I knew Renato from Paris. He was a friend of Picasso—I told him what had happened, and I asked, "Where are you going, for God's sake?" We had to talk in shorthand in French, which she didn't speak. Renato told me then, Lisbon.

So I landed at the Mexican consulate and there were a bunch of Mexicans I'd never seen. I asked them if Renato was there, and they said, No, they didn't know when he'd be in. I told them I was going to stay and wait. They protested, "Señorita, but . . ." This and that. So I said, "The police are after me." Which was more or less true. So they said, "In that case . . ." Wink, wink. "You can wait for Renato."

The ambassador was wonderful with me later. I must have gone in to see him, and he said, "You're on Mexican territory. Even the English can't touch you." I don't know when Renato appeared. Eventually, he said, "We're going to have to get married. I know it's awful for both of us, as we don't believe in this sort of thing, but . . ."

At that time I was as frightened of my family as of the Germans. I'd found Renato attractive when I first met him, and I still found him very attractive. He had a dark face like an Indian's and very white hair. No, I felt perfectly sane. I was just feeling that I would do anything not to be sent to Africa, not to fall in with my family's plans.

Then Max appeared, with Peggy [Guggenheim] and we were always together, all of us. It was a very weird thing, with everybody's children, and ex-husbands and ex-wives [Laurence Vail was there, Peggy Guggenheim's former husband, with his new wife, Kay Boyle]. I felt there was something very wrong in Max's being with Peggy. I knew he didn't love Peggy, and I still have this very puritanical streak, that you mustn't be with anyone you don't love. But Peggy is very maligned. She was rather a noble person, generous, and she never ever was unpleasant. She offered to pay for my airplane to New York, so I could go with them. But I didn't want that. I was with Renato, and eventually, we went by boat to New York, where I stayed for almost a year, until we left for Mexico.

That was the story.

My mother came to Mexico when my son Pablo was born in 1946. But we never talked about this time. It's the sort of thing English people of that generation didn't discuss. That was one side of my mother's peculiar and rather complex character.

One would have thought they would have come themselves to Santander. But you know, they didn't. Nanny was sent. You can imagine how much Spanish Nanny talked. It's a wonder she ever got there. What is terrible is that one's anger is stifled. I never really got angry. I felt I didn't really have time. I was tormented by the idea that I had to paint, and when I was away from Max and first with Renato, I painted immediately.

I never saw my father again.

—As told to Marina Warner
July 1987, New York

A Note on the Texts

The texts in this volume were established by the author, in consultation with Marina Warner and Paul De Angelis, in 1987. The English-language texts (*Little Francis* and *Down Below*) had never been formally prepared for publication before, and indeed this is the first publication of *Little Francis* in its original language anywhere. Nor had any English translation of the French texts (*La Maison de la peur* and *La Dame ovale*) been reviewed by the author. Every attempt was made to remain true to the spirit and tone of the author's first-draft compositions of 1937–1943, while minor revisions were made for the sake of clarity and accuracy.

Here are composition, publication, and translation information on the texts:

La Maison de la peur (The House of Fear). Written 1937–38, in French. Published in Paris as a pamphlet in

1938, without corrections in French spelling, by Henri Parisot. Included three illustrations by Max Ernst. First edition: 120 copies. English translations of *Preface to The House of Fear* and *The House of Fear* by Kathrine Talbot with Marina Warner.

La Dame ovale (The Oval Lady). Written 1937–38, in French. Published in Paris in 1939 by Editions G.L.M. Included seven collages by Max Ernst. First edition: 535 copies. English translations of *The Oval Lady, The Debutante, The Royal Summons, A Man in Love,* and *Uncle Sam Carrington* by Kathrine Talbot with Marina Warner.

Little Francis. Written 1937–38, in English, in Saint-Martin-d'Ardèche. First published in French, under the title *Histoire du Petit Francis,* in a version edited and translated by Jacqueline Chénieux, as part of a collection entitled *Pigeon Vole.* Editions Le Temps Qu'il Fait, Cognac, France, 1986. First edition: 1,000 copies.

Down Below. Written in English (text now lost), dictated in French to Jeanne Megnen, in 1943. First published in *VVV*, No. 4, February 1944, in a translation from the French by Victor Llona. The original French dictation was published by Editions Fontaine, Paris, 1946. Both the French dictation and the Victor Llona translation were used as the basis for the text here, which was reviewed and revised for factual accuracy by the author, who added the postscript in an interview with Marina Warner.